She was full ~~of~~
thought in son~~e~~

So much for the in~~nocent~~ ~~~~
girl without a scrap of make-up! What he saw
in front of him was a dead sexy little buttercup
blonde. She was wearing a swishy blue dress
that doubled the impact of her violet eyes. He
hadn't expected this transformation. He was so
astounded he had trouble hiding it.

"Have a problem with the way I look, Daniel?"
she asked sweetly, pleased at his readable
reaction.

"No, ma'am." He half shrugged. "You look
different, that's all." Daniel studied her face.
"What's the problem?"

"I'm sick with nerves, if you must know."

"I promise I'll lay down my life for you." He
said it lightly. Then it struck him. He had just
said something that he actually *meant*.

Dear Reader

It is with much pleasure that I welcome you to my four-book mini-series, **Men of the Outback**. The setting moves from my usual stamping ground, my own state of Queensland, to the Northern Territory, which is arguably the most colourful and exciting part of the continent. It comprises what we call the Top End and the Red Centre—two extreme climatic and geographical divisions. This is what makes the Territory so fascinating. The tropical World Heritage-listed Kakadu National Park, with crocodiles and water buffalo to the Top, and in the Centre the desert, the 'Dead Heart'—not actually dead at all, only lying dormant until the rains transform it into the greatest garden on earth.

The pervading theme of the series is family. Family offers endless opportunities for its members to hurt and be hurt, to love and support, or bitterly condemn. What sort of family we grew up in reverberates for the rest of our lives. One thing is certain: at the end of the day, *blood* binds.

I invite you, dear reader, to explore the lives of my families. My warmest best wishes to you all.

Margaret Way

Men of the Outback

THE CATTLEMAN (part of *To Mum With Love*)
THE CATTLE BARON'S BRIDE
HER OUTBACK PROTECTOR

Look out for Cecile's story. Coming soon.

HER OUTBACK
PROTECTOR

BY
MARGARET WAY

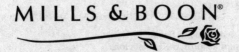

MILLS & BOON®

First published in Great Britain 2006
Harlequin Mills & Boon Limited,
Eton House, 18-24 Paradise Road, Richmond, Surrey TW9 1SR

© Margaret Way, Pty., Ltd 2006

ISBN 0 263 84902 3

Set in Times Roman 11½ on 14 pt.
02-0606-55942

Printed and bound in Spain
by Litografia Rosés, S.A., Barcelona

CHAPTER ONE

Darwin Airport
The Northern Territory
Australia

INSIDE the domestic terminal Daniel surveyed the swirling crowd. A full head and shoulders over most people he had an excellent view over the sea of bobbing heads. He was confident he'd spot the girl, technically his boss. There were tourists galore. Most were probably headed for the World Heritage listed great national park, Kakadu, but many of the faces in the crowd were familiar; Territorians returning from a stint in the big coastal cities of the eastern seaboard; business, pleasure, maybe both. Striding along to the check-in counter, where his charge had agreed to be, a booklet on the Northern Territory in hand, he constantly exchanged waves and friendly calls. He was a familiar figure himself after nearly six years of working for Rigby Kingston, a pioneer cattleman recently deceased.

His allotted chore for the day was picking up Kingston's long estranged granddaughter, Alexandra, and
ferrying her back to the station.

She could have flown to Alice Springs. That
would have been a lot closer to Moondai. It was a
bit of a haul from Darwin in the tropical Top End of
the Territory to Moondai in the Red Centre but he'd
managed to kill two birds with the one stone,
dropping his leading hand off at RDH, the Royal
Darwin Hospital, for a deferred minor op and
picking up the girl who had made the long trip from
Brisbane. But surely even a city girl would appreci-
ate the magnificent spectacle of great stretches of the
Top End under water? That was what she was going
to see. Vast swathes of floodplains teeming with
nomadic water birds; chains of billabongs floating
armadas of exquisite multicoloured waterlilies; the
western fringe of Kakadu, the North, East and West
Alligator Rivers snaking through the jungle. That
stupendous panorama, especially the endless vistas
of waterlilies and the thundering waterfalls of the
Wet were to him as much an enduring image of the
Top End as were the crocodiles.

They were into March now. The Wet, the *Gune-
meleng* as the aboriginals called it, was all but over.
Two cyclones had threatened the tropical North, one
extremely dangerous. It had put Darwin, destroyed
in Cyclone Tracy in 1974, on high alert. Mercifully
cyclone Ingrid had taken herself off into the Timor

Sea, but not before dumping torrential rain over the coast and the hinterland. That same deluge, more than they had seen in decades, had brought life-giving water to the Red Centre. The Finke, the oldest river on earth, ninety-nine per cent of the time dry, was now flowing bank to bank. These days it thrilled him to fly over it rejoicing in all the waterfalls that ran off the ochre coloured rock faces into serene green gullies.

Born in tropical North Queensland not far from the mighty Daintree rain forest he had become used to the desert environment. It was very, very special. Maybe the girl would think so, too. After all she had been born on Moondai and spent enough years there to remember it.

"Dan!" A voice boomed.

A passenger off the Brisbane-Darwin flight, a big affable looking man, pushing sixty with keen blue eyes threw out an arm. It was Bill Morrissey, a well respected member of the Northern Territory Administration.

"How are you, sir?" Respect and liking showed in Daniel's face.

They shook hands. "Hot and tired." Morrissey wiped his forehead with a spotless white handkerchief. "What brings you into Darwin?"

No harm in telling him. "I'm here to pick up Alexandra Kingston and deliver her to her family."

"Lordy!" Morrissey put a hand to his fast thinning

hair as though to check it was still there. "Wouldn't like to be that poor child! Not with those relatives. Rigby's will would have totally alienated his son and grandson and let's not forget the second wife, Elsa. I have to see it as an angry man's last response. Rigby cut his family out of the main game even when it's a fact of life dynasties die out without sons to take over. Daughters tend to walk off with some guy out of the family field."

"True," Daniel acknowledged, having witnessed that scenario first-hand. "But in all fairness to Mr. Kingston, Lloyd and Berne aren't cut out to be cattlemen. Maybe Mr. Kingston made demands on them they simply couldn't cope with, but they have no taste for the job on their own admission."

"Well, they could never be carbon copies of him," Morrissey replied. "A lot of rich families produce at least a couple of offspring who have no head for big business. Now the girl's father, Trevor, *was* shaping up to be a chip off the old block. Tragedy he was killed. It happens in our way of life. You're still going to be around, though, aren't you, Dan? Can't see how they could possibly do without you. You might be young, but you're up there with the best."

Daniel heard the sincerity in the older man's voice. "Thanks for the vote of confidence, sir. I'm committed to one year at least under the terms of Mr. Kingston's will."

Morrissey clamped a hand on his shoulder. "Trust

Rigby to ensure the transition would be smooth. With you at the helm, or guiding the girl into getting a professional manager they might be able to get by. How old are you now, son? Twenty-seven, twenty-eight?"

"Twenty-eight." Sometimes it seemed to Daniel he had to be at least double that age, he had seen so much of life.

"Do you have any idea how well regarded you are?"

Daniel gave his very appealing, crooked grin. "If I am I'm very glad. I've worked hard."

"That you have!" Morrissey agreed, knowing the full story. "Rigby certainly thought so and we all know how demanding he was."

"He wasn't loved, that's for sure!" Daniel agreed wryly, "but I always found him fair enough and willing to *listen*. One of the things that made him so successful I guess. He never had a closed mind, even for a relative newcomer to the game like me. Besides I've learned to love the Territory. It's my home now."

"And the Territory needs young men like you," Morrissey said, comfortable with the mantle of mentor. "Young men of brains and vision. You've got both." He thrust out his hand for a final shake. "Best go now. Can't keep the chauffeur waiting. When you're next in Darwin come and see me. When your twelve months are up I guarantee I'll find you something to suit your talents."

"Might hold you to that, sir." Daniel grinned.

Morrissey began to move away, then paused, looking back. "By the way, Joel Moreland has expressed a desire to meet you. Not for the first time I might add. The Big Man's heard about you. Now he wants to take a good *look* at you. You could be in luck, there, my boy. Moreland is a Territory icon. I'll set it up for lunch. Just the three of us."

"That's great!" Daniel was surprised and deeply flattered. It never hurt to have friends in high places he thought as he strode off. Joel Moreland was known in the Territory as the man with the Midas touch. Not one of his many ventures stretching back forty years and more had failed. Not that the man with the Midas touch hadn't known his own tragedy. Moreland's son and heir, Jared, had been killed in a freak accident at an Alice Springs rodeo well over twenty years before. Apparently he had put his own life on the line to save a cavorting teenager from a maddened bullock. The Grim Reaper no more spared the lives of those rolling in money than he did the poor.

Well *he* knew all about being poor but strangely he'd never developed any lasting complexes about it. He was a fighter. He'd spent much of his childhood fighting for the honour of his pretty little mother and the good name some callous guy had stripped from her without looking back. People didn't label the illegitimate *bastards* any more. It was politically incorrect. When he was a kid growing up in a small, redneck Queensland town, they didn't give a fig about that.

From very humble beginnings he had made something of himself. He'd had help. Everyone needs a little help. Even the strongest couldn't do it on their own. A Channel Country cattleman called Harry Cunningham had given him and his mother that helping hand when they were so down on their luck he'd been filled with fear his vulnerable mother would resort to taking her own life. Harry Cunningham had been their saviour, the man behind his education.

"You've got to have an education, Dan. You're smart as they come, but education is everything. Get it. Then you can pay me back."

Well he had paid Harry back, reviving the fortunes of Harry's run-down station only to have Harry's daughter, his only child, sell the valuable property within a month. Some sons-in-law proved themselves to be eminently capable as substitute sons but as Bill Morrissey had pointed out this particular daughter had married a city slicker who had shied away violently from the prospect of taking on a cattle station. Far easier to take the money and run.

It was Harry's glowing recommendations that had come to the ears of his late employer, Rigby Kingston. That's what had gained him a job on Moondai, rising to the rank of overseer. It was *he* Rigby Kingston had looked to. Not his remaining son, Lloyd, or Lloyd's son, Bernard. It wasn't often a man bypassed the males of his family to leave the bulk of his estate to a granddaughter, moreover one who had been banished. What was his reasoning? Did Kingston secretly want his heirs to *fail?* Having been robbed of his favourite son, Trevor, the girl's father, the rest could go to hell? Rigby Kingston had been a very *curious* man. Yet tyrannical old Kingston had left him, Daniel Carson, a nobody, however dramatically he had risen, a handy little nest egg of $250,000, on top of his salary, on the proviso he remain on Moondai as overseer for a period of twelve months after Kingston's demise.

It was all so damned *bizarre!*

It didn't take him a minute more to spot the Kingston heiress. All five feet two of her. Her slight figure, standing brolga-like on one leg, was a few feet from the check-in counter, booklet on the Territory in hand. He didn't know what he had been expecting. An ultra smooth city girl in expensive designer gear. There were plenty of them about. It surely wasn't *this!* A cute little teenager—okay she was twenty, nearly twenty-one, but what the heck, she didn't look a day over sixteen and she was showing at least five or six inches of baby smooth skin between the end of her T-shirt and the top of her tight jeans. He took in the delicate coltish limbs, jeans sinking on nonexistent hips, the T-shirt blue with a silver logo on the front of her delicate breasts, gentle little rises beneath the clingy fabric. She shifted one hand in her hip pocket, apparently searching for something but as he closed in on her she raised her cropped head and literally *jumped*.

What the hell! He wasn't such a dangerous looking character, *was* he? Maybe his hair was overly long. It was very thick and it grew at a helluva rate and there weren't too many hairdressers around Moondai. He had lived with his image so long he couldn't really tell how he presented. Perhaps seen through those saucer eyes staring at him he looked a touch wild; eyes that were so big and radiant a blue they dwarfed her other small features. Except maybe the mouth. Not a trace of lipstick so far as he could see, but then makeup was a mystery to him, but beautifully shaped. He had a notion he was staring back, but she was *such* a surprise packet.

Obviously she didn't agree with the notion that a woman's hair was her crowning glory, either. Hers was cut to within an inch of its life. Buttercup-yellow, curling in the humid heat into a cap of pretty petals. A few escaped onto her forehead. What was the definition of sexy for God's sake? Against all the odds Miss Alexandra Kingston, looking like she wasn't all that long out of school, fell into that category.

He collected himself enough to tip a jaunty forefinger to the brim of his black akubra. It felt like he *towered* over her all the more so because he was wearing high heeled riding boots. He scrutinised her shoes, soft moccasin kind of thing. "Ms Kingston?" he asked, trying to keep all trace of dryness out of his voice and not succeeding all that well.

"Sandra, please." She cleared a husky throat. "No one calls me Ms Kingston." Her hand rose defensively to her neat little skull as though to check on an unfamiliar hair style.

Probably just cut it, he thought. Unceremoniously with a pair of nail scissors like an expression of rebellion.

"I *am* an employee," he pointed out.

"Hey." She shrugged. "I said you can call me Sandra."

"How very egalitarian. Dan Carson." He introduced himself. "I'm your overseer on Moondai and your chauffeur for the day. I'm here to transport you to the station."

"Transport?"

He saw her gulp. "Now why make it sound like you're going on a road train?" he chided gently. Road trains that transported anything from great numbers of cattle to petrol were an awesome sight on Outback roads.

"I was worried about the word, *transport*," she said smartly.

Her voice all of a sudden had an unexpected *bite* to it, an *adultness* that had him re-evaluating her. "Set your mind at rest. We go by helicopter," he told her. Could there be a trace of *hostility* in those bluer than blue eyes? "I had to drop my leading hand into RDH for a minor op so it was convenient to pick you up and bring you home."

"How kind." The expressive voice turned sweetly acid. "Only Moondai's no home of mine, Mr. Carson."

"Please—Daniel." He dipped his head. "I'm not in *my* element with Mr. Carson."

"Great! I'm glad we've got that sorted out."

So it *was* antagonism.

"Actually I thought Christian names might be beneath you." She was desperate to cover up the fact she felt as if she'd been struck by lightning. Daniel Carson, her overseer, was a marvellous looking guy with Action and Adventure emblazoned all over him. He'd make the perfect hero in some epic movie, she thought. Dark, swashbuckling good looks, splendid body, commanding height. The aura was *mesmerising*, but his manner was definitely nonthreatening.

"Nothing so old-fashioned," he mocked gently, looking towards the luggage carousel. It was ringed by passengers all staring fixedly towards the chute as though willpower alone would cause the luggage to start tumbling through. Every last one appeared to be in a desperate hurry to be somewhere else. "The baggage hasn't started to arrive as yet," he commented, unnecessarily, just making conversation. "How many pieces do you have?"

"Just the one," she murmured, so overloaded by his presence, she transferred her attention to the milling crowd. Multiracial. Multilingual. English predominated; a variety of accents, Aussie, Pommie, New Zealander, American. Lots of backpackers. A group of handsome Germans, speaking their own language, which she had studied for four years at high school; Italian, Greek, Scandinavian, ethnic groups from all over the South-East Asia region.

As the gateway into Australia, Darwin, named in honour of Charles Darwin, the famous British naturalist, was a real melting pot; a far more cosmopolitan city than her home base, Brisbane. In fact it had the *feel* and even the smell of Asia. Hot, my God, how hot and such *humid* air! Almost equatorial but somehow vibrant, the scent of jasmine, joss sticks, spices; beautiful golden skinned Asian girls, dead straight shining hair sliding down their backs, strolling by in little bra tops with tiny shorts, a trio of older Asian women wearing gorgeous silk tunics over trousers.

She saw her overseer, Dan Carson, pause to smile at an attractive flight attendant who came over all giggly and flushing. Who could blame her, Sandra thought, wanting to put an instant stop to it. "Hi, Dan!"

"Hi, Abby!" His eyes eventually moved back to Sandra's small censorious face. Mentally he began to rearrange his first impressions. Young she might be, but she was as sharp as a tack. "You believe in travelling light?"

"Surely it's one of the great virtues," she told him

loftily, shocked by that irrational flash of jealousy. Where in the world had *that* come from?

He digested this by compressing his quirky mouth. "Not especially in women. They generally travel with mountains of luggage."

"You'd know, would you?" Another haughty look as like a replay, two more attendants smiled and wiggled their fingers at him while he grinned back, saluting them with a forefinger to the broad brim of his hat already tipped rakishly over his eyes. Not only her overseer but a playboy of sorts though there was something almost mischievous in those grins.

"I'd say so." He turned back to her.

He used that flashing, faintly crooked white smile like a sex aid she thought looking on him sternly. "Well I'm not staying long."

"How totally unexpected." He couldn't keep the mockery out of a baritone that flowed like molasses. "Seeing you've inherited the station and all."

Sandra's eyes glowed the blue of a gas flame. "So what are you saying, that's *amazing?*"

He shrugged. "No more than if you said you'd climbed the Matterhorn on your own. Still, I'm sure your grandfather had his reasons."

She gave a cracked laugh. "He did. He hated me. Now he's gone he wants Moondai to go to wrack and ruin. Then again, my grandfather never could miss an opportunity to cheat the family out of their expectations. How did he come to hire *you?*" She met his eyes squarely, not bothering to conceal the challenge. "Surely there's Uncle Lloyd and cousin Bernie to take charge?"

"Both of whom prefer a different lifestyle," he returned blandly. "No, actually the job got dumped on me."

"You don't sound as though you expect to lose it any time soon?" she cut in.

Pretty perceptive! "Now this is the tricky bit," he explained. "Under the terms of your grandfather's will I can't check out for at least twelve months."

"What?" She rammed both hands into her jeans pockets. Her waist was so tiny he knew he could span it with his two hands.

"You didn't know about it?" The way she tossed her head reminded him of a high stepping filly.

"My mind went blank after the first few minutes of hearing the will read."

"Pays to listen," he commented briefly. "Ah, the baggage is starting to come through. Let's go." He grabbed hold of her soft leather hold-all and slung it over his shoulder. "You can point out which suitcase is yours when it arrives. Or is it a backpack?"

"It's a designer case," she said flatly.

"Sweet Lord!" Try as he might he couldn't prevent a laugh.

"Envious?"

"Not at all."

"You'll be happy to know it's not mine," she said waspishly. "A friend of mine lent it to me."

"That surely means your friend likes you?" he asked, amused by their disproportionate heights. She was a *tiny* little thing. He could fit her into his back pocket.

"He *loves* me." She stared straight ahead, almost trotting to keep up with him and his long, long legs.

"Loves you?" he repeated, as though amazed she was ready for romantic love. "Would this friend be your fiancé?"

"He's gay," she said quite patiently, considering how she felt. Outside, all mock toughness and tart banter. Inside, a throbbing bundle of nerves.

Daniel took up a position beside the carousel as the throng miraculously parted for him like the Red Sea for Moses.

"He's nearly eighty," she continued, trying to keep her attention on the circling luggage when she felt like flopping in a heap. It had been a long, long trip from Brisbane. Another one faced her. She was terrified of light aircraft and helicopters. With good reason. "He has his Abyssinian cat, Sheba, and he has me. We're neighbours and good friends."

"So where do you live?" he asked mock politely, lifting a hand to acknowledge yet another enthusiastic wave from the far side of the luggage carousel.

All these women trying to communicate with *her* overseer, instead of getting on with their business.

Sandra fumed. She didn't feel in the least good humoured about it. An attractive redhead this time, who seemed to have peeled off most of her clothes in favour of coolness. It was irritating all this outrageous flirtation.

"You don't need to know," she told him severely. "But I'm desperately missing my flat already."

"Like the older man do you?" he asked, rather amused by her huffiness. It was fair to say she didn't *look* like a considerable heiress. She didn't dress like one, either. She was definitely *not* friendly when he was long used to easy smiles from women.

"The older the better," she said with emphasis. "You seem awfully young to be overseer of a big station?" She eyed him critically. He radiated such *energy* it needed to be channelled.

"I grew up *fast*," he answered bluntly. "I had a very rough childhood."

"That's hard to believe." He really was absurdly good-looking. Hunk was the word. Stunning if you liked the cocky macho male always ready for the next conquest. "You look like you were born to the sound of hundreds of champagne corks popping…already astride your own pony by the time you were two."

He smiled grimly. "You're way off." He watched the expensive suitcase tumble out onto the conveyor belt, getting exactly the same treatment as the most humble label.

"So there's a story?" Why wouldn't there be? He looked anything but dull.

"Isn't there always? *You've* got one." He pinned her with a glance and a rather elegantly raised eyebrow.

"Haven't I just." There was a forlornness in her eyes before the covers came down.

He hefted her heavy suitcase like it was a bundle of goose down. "Listen, how are you feeling?" he asked, noticing she had suddenly lost colour.

"Quite awful since you ask!"

Such a tart response but he didn't hold it against her. "Did you have anything to eat on the plane?"

Dammit if he didn't have a dimple in one cheek. "A big steak," she answered in the same sarcastic vein. "Actually I had an orange juice. Plane food lacks subtlety don't you think? Besides, I hate planes. I thought I might throw up. I didn't really want to precipitate a crisis."

He pondered for half a second. "Why don't we grab something to eat now?" he suggested. "There are a couple of places to grab coffee and a sandwich. Come to think of it I'm hungry, too."

She didn't bother to argue. He was used to taking charge as well. He didn't even consult her about what she wanted but saw her seated then walked over to the counter to order.

Two waitresses, one with a terrible hair day, sped towards him so quickly, the younger one, scowling darkly, was forced to fall back to avoid being muscled aside. No matter where you were good-looking guys managed to get served first, Sandra thought disgustedly.

Macho Man returned a few minutes later with a laden tray. "This might help you feel better," he said, obviously trying to jolly her up.

"Thank you." She tried to fix a smile on her face, but she was feeling too grim.

He placed a frothy cappuccino with a good crema in front of her, a plate of sandwiches and a couple of tempting little pastries. "We can share. There's ham and whole grain mustard or chicken and avocado."

"I don't really care."

He rolled his eyes. "Eat up," he scolded, exactly like a big brother. "You're not anorexic are you?" He surveyed her with glinting eyes. "Not as I understand it, anorexics admit to it."

"I eat plenty," she said coolly, beginning to tuck away.

"Pleased to hear it." He pushed the plate of sandwiches closer to her. "What did you do to your hair, if it's not a rude question? Obviously it's by your own hand, not a day at the hairdressers?"

To his consternation her huge beautiful eyes turned into overflowing blue lagoons.

It made him feel really bad. "Look, I'm sorry," he apologised hastily, remorse written all across his

strongly hewn features. "You have a right to wear
your hair any way you choose. It actually looks
kinda cute and it must be cool?"

She dashed the back of her hand across her eyes
and took a gulp of air. This big macho guy looked so
contrite she had an urge to tell him. A spur of the
moment thing when she'd barely been able to speak
of it. "A little friend of mine died recently of leukaemia," she said, her expression a mix of grief and tenderness. "She was only seven. When she lost all her
beautiful curly hair, I cut mine off to be supportive.
Afterwards the two of us laughed and cried our-
selves silly at how we looked."

He glanced away, his throat tight. "Now that's
the saddest story in the world, Alexandra."

"You just want to die yourself."

"I know."

The sympathy and understanding in his voice
soothed her.

"But your little friend wouldn't want that," he
continued. "She'd want you to go on and make
something of your life. Maybe you even owe it to
her. What was her name?"

"Nicole." She swallowed hard, determined not
to break down. She could never ever go through
something so heartbreaking again. "Everyone
called her Nikki."

"I'm sorry." He sounded sad and respectful.

She liked him for that. It was oddly comforting

considering he was a perfect stranger. "The death of
a child has to be one of the worst things in life," he
mused. "The death of a child, a parent, a beloved
spouse."

A sentiment Sandra shared entirely. She nodded,
for the first time allowing herself to stare into his
eyes. He had the most striking colouring there was.
Light eyes, darn near silver, fringed by long, thick,
jet-black lashes any woman would die for. Jet-
black rather wildly curling hair to match. It kicked
up in waves on the nape. Strong arched brows,
gleaming dark copper skin, straight nose, beautifully structured chin and jaw. For all the polished
gleam of health on his skin she knew his beard
would *rasp*. She could almost *feel* it, unable to
control the little shudder that ran down her spine.
He was the sort of guy who looked like he could
handle himself anywhere, which she supposed
would add to his attractiveness to women. A real
plus for her, however, was that he could be *kind*.
Kindness was much more important than drop dead
good looks.

"I know what loss is all about," he said, after a
moment of silence, absently stirring three teaspoons
of raw sugar into his coffee. "There are stages one
after the other. You have to learn to slam down barri-
ers."

"Is that what you did?" Her voice quickened with
interest, even as she removed the sugar. Obviously

he had a sweet tooth and too much sugar wasn't good for his health.

"Had to," he said. "Grief can drain all the life out of you when our job is to go on. So how old are you anyway?" He tried a more bantering tone to ease the rather painful tension. "My first thought was about sixteen," he said, not altogether joking.

"Try again." She bit into another sandwich. They were *good*. Plenty of filling on fresh multi-grain bread.

"Okay I know you're twenty." He concentrated on her intriguing face with her hair now all fluffed up.

"Nearly twenty-one." She picked up another sandwich. "Or I will be in six months time when I inherit. If I'm still alive, that is. Once I'm on Moondai and at the mercy of my relatives who knows?"

He set his cup down so sharply, a few heads turned to see if he'd cracked the saucer. "You can't be serious?"

"Dead serious," she confirmed. "My mother and I left Moondai when I was ten, nearly eleven. She was a basket case. I went into a frenzy of bad behaviour that lasted for years. I was chucked out of two schools but that's another story. We left not long after my dad, Trevor, was killed. Do you know how he was killed?"

"I'd like you to tell me." Obviously she had to talk to someone about it. Like him, she appeared to have much bottled up.

"He crashed in the Cessna."

He sat staring at her. "I know. I'm sorry."

Her great eyes glittered. "Did your informant tell you the Cessna was sabotaged?"

"Dear oh dear!" He shook his head in sad disbelief.

"Don't dear oh dear me!" she cried emotionally. Clearly her beliefs were tearing her to pieces. "Sandra, let it go," he advised quietly. "There was an inquiry. The wreckage would have been gone over by experts. There was no question of foul play. Who would want to do such a thing anyway?"

She took a deep gulp of her coffee. It was too hot. It burnt her mouth. She swore softly. "You may think you're smart—you may even *be* smart—I'm sure you have to be to run Moondai, but that was a damned silly question, Daniel Carson. Who was the person with the most to gain?"

He looked at her sharply. "God, you don't think very highly of your uncle, do you?"

"Do you?"

"My job is to run the station, not criticise your family."

Tension was all over her. "So we're on different sides?"

"Do we have to be?" He looked into her eyes. A man could dive into those sparkling blue lagoons and come out refreshed.

"I don't *want* Moondai," she said, shaking her shorn head.

"So who are you going to pass it on to, *me?*" He tried a smile.

She sighed deeply. "I'd just as soon leave it to a total stranger as my family."

"That includes cousin Berne?"

She put both elbows on the table. "He was a dreadful kid," she announced, her eyes darkening with bad memories. "He was always giving me Chinese burns but I never did let him see me cry. Worse, he used to kick my cat, Olly. We had to leave her behind which was terrible. As for me, I could look after myself and I could run fast. I bet he's no better now than I remember?"

"You'll have to see for yourself, Alexandra." He kept his tone deliberately neutral.

"I won't have one single friend inside that house," she said then shut up abruptly, biting her lip.

He didn't like that idea. "I work for you, Sandra," he told her, underscoring *work*. "If you need someone you can trust you should consider me."

She continued to nibble on her full bottom lip, something he found *very* distracting. "I certainly won't have anyone else. I wasn't going to offload my troubles onto you, not this early anyway, but I'm a mite scared of my folks."

He was shocked. "But, Sandra, no one is going to harm you." Even as he said it, his mind stirred with anxiety. The Kingstons were a weird lot, but surely not homicidal. Then again Rigby Kingston had left an estate worth roughly sixty million. The girl stood between it and them. Not a comfortable position to be in.

Frustrated by his attitude, Sandra dredged up an old Outback expression. "What would you know, you big galah!"

He choked back a laugh. "Hey, mind who you're calling names!"

"Sorry. Galah is not the word for you. You're more an eagle. But surely you realise they must have been shocked out of their minds by the will. Uncle Lloyd would have fully expected to inherit. He wouldn't want to work the place. He'd sell it. Bernie would go along with that. Bernie disliked anything to do with station work. You must know that, too. Where do you live?" she asked abruptly.

"I have the overseer's bungalow."

"Roy Sommerville, what happened to him? He was the overseer when we left."

"Died a couple of years back of lung cancer. He was of the generation that chain smoked from dawn to dark."

"Poor old Roy! He was nice to me."

"Anyone would be nice to you." His response was involuntary.

She grimaced. "I don't recall Uncle Lloyd ever bouncing me on his knee. His ex-wife, Aunty Jilly, used to dodge me and my mother all the time. No wonder that marriage didn't work out. Bernie was always so darn nasty. Now they must all think I'm the worst thing that ever happened."

He couldn't deny that. "What was your grandfather like with you?" he asked, really wanting to know. "Any fond memories?"

"Hello, we're talking Rigby Kingston here!" she chortled. "The most rambunctious old son of a bitch to ride out of the Red Centre."

He shook his head. "When you'd melt any man's heart." A major paradox here when Kingston had left her his fortune.

"I don't *want* to melt men's hearts," she exploded, the blood flowing into her cheeks. "It's all smiles and kisses one day. Rude shocks the next. I don't like men at all. They don't bring out the best in me."

He held back a sigh. "I think you must have had some bad experiences."

"You can say that again! But to get back to my dear old grandpop who remembered me at the end, I do recall a few pats on the head. A tweak of the curls before he was out the front door. I didn't bother him anyway. He was happy enough when my dad was alive. After that, he turned into the Grandad from Hell. He seemed to put the blame for what happened to my dad on my mother."

"How could *she* have been responsible?" he asked, puzzled.

"Uncle Lloyd blew the whistle on a little affair she

had in Sydney," she told him bleakly. "Mum used to go away a lot and leave Dad and me at Moondai. Uncle Lloyd said she was really *wild,* but then he was a great one for airing everyone else's dirty linen." She broke off, staring at him accusingly. "You must have heard all this?"

Why pretend he hadn't when an unbelievable number of people had made it their business to fill him in on Pamela Kingston's alleged exploits? Lloyd Kingston wasn't the only one who liked airing the world's dirty linen. Apparently Sandra's mother had been famous for being not only radiantly beautiful but something of a two-timing Jezebel. There had even been gossip about who Alexandra's father really was. Alexandra didn't look a bit like a Kingston which now that he had seen her Dan had to concede. The Kingstons were dark haired, dark eyed, *tall* people with no sense of humour. Pamela had routinely been labelled as an absentee wife and mother who spent half her time in Sydney and Melbourne living it up and getting her photo in all the glossy magazines. Dan knew she had remarried eighteen months after her first husband's death. Wedding number two was no fairy tale, either. It too had gone on the rocks. Pamela was currently married to her third husband, a merchant banker with whom she had a young son. It seemed Sandra had moved out fairly early. He wondered exactly *when?* Not yet twenty-one the combative little Ms Sandra

Kingston gave the strong impression she had looked after herself for some time. And possibly after her mother, the basket case. Hell, he knew as much about female depression and the various forms it took as the illustrious Dr. Freud.

"All right, what are you thinking about?" Sandra cut into Dan's pondering.

"I was wondering when you left home?"

At the question put so probingly she began to move the salt and pepper shakers around like chess pieces. "To be perfectly honest, from which you might deduce I'm given to telling lies—I'm *not*—I've never really had a home."

"You and me both," he confessed, laconically.

Instantly she was diverted from her own sombre thoughts. "So there's more?" She leaned forward, elbows on the table, all attention.

"If you think I'm about to share my life story with you, Ms Kingston, I'm not!"

She shook her head. "Is that a hint *I'm* communicating too much?" she asked tartly, slumping back in her chair.

"Not at all. It strikes me you've spent a lot of time alone?"

She sighed theatrically, then stole one of his sandwiches. "That's what happens when your mother has had three husbands."

"One of them was your dad," he pointed out.

She nearly choked she was so quick to retort.

"That son of a bitch Lloyd challenged that at least a dozen times before I was ten.'"

The muscles along his jaw tightened. He knew all about labels. "He's not a very nice person," he said shortly.

"He's a bully," she said. "And I'm going to prove that. He really *really* upset my mother. I know she wasn't the woman to exercise caution but don't you think she would have been completely insane to try to put one across my dad let alone my fearsome old grandpop. My dad always knew I was his little girl. He used to call me 'my little possum.' He told me every day he loved me. I think he was the only person in the entire world who did. Then he went off and left me. I was so sad and so angry. My mum and I *needed* him. It's awful to be on your own." She dug her pretty white teeth into her nether lip again, dragging them across the cushiony surface, colouring it rosy.

"So a man does come in handy?" he asked.

She looked into his eyes and he saw the sorrow behind the prickly front. "A dad is really important."

Hadn't he faced that all his life? Even a bastard of a dad.

"Getting killed was the very last thing your dad *wanted,* Sandra. Unfortunately death is the *one* appointment none of us can break. I'm sure your mother loves you. Your grandfather too in his own way."

"God that's corny!" Now she fixed him with a contemptuous glare. "In his *own* way. What a cop-out!"

"He made you his heiress," he pointed out reasonably. "Do people who hate you actually leave you a fortune? I don't think so. Your grandfather bypassed his son, your uncle, and his only grandson who is older than you by three years."

"I can count," she said shortly, hungrily polishing off another one of his sandwiches. "I actually got to go to university. I was a famous swot."

"Head never out of a book?"

"Something like that." She shrugged, picking away a piece of rocket. "In a locked room. My stepfather, Jeremy Linklatter, IV, developed a few little unlawful ideas about me."

He who thought himself unshockable was shocked to the core.

"You can't trust anyone these days," she said in a world-weary fashion. "Certainly not men. There should be a Protection Scheme for female stepchildren."

"Hell!" he breathed, hoping it wasn't going to get worse. "He didn't touch you?"

Her expression showed her detestation of stepfather Jeremy. "Not the bad stuff." How was she confiding all this to a stranger when she had never spoken about it at all? There was just something about this Daniel Carson.

"Thank God for that!" He released a pent-up sigh. "The guy must have crawled out from under a rock. So when did you leave home?"

She shrugged, licking a little bit of avocado off her fingertip. "I went to boarding school. Then I went on to uni and had on campus accommodation. It proved a lot safer than being at home."

"Did your mother know what was going on?" Surely not. That would have been criminal.

She sighed. "My mother only sees what she wants to see. She can't help it. It's the way she's made. Besides, Jem was pretty adept at picking his moments. I was always on high alert. Occasionally he got in an awful messy kiss or a grope. Once I pinched his face so hard he cried out. Then I took to carrying a weapon on my person."

He could picture it. "Don't tell me. A stun gun?"

"Close. A needle with a tranquilliser in it."

"You're joking!" That was totally unexpected. And dangerous.

"All right, I am. But I was desperate. I took to carrying my dad's Swiss Army knife. You know what that is?"

"Of course I know what it is," he said, frowning hard at the very idea of her needing to carry such a thing as a weapon. "I have one, like millions of other guys. It's a miniature tool box."

"You don't have one like mine. It's a collector's item," she boasted. "An original 1891 version."

"Really? I'd like to see it."

She laughed. "And I'd enjoy showing it to you only I couldn't bring it on the plane."

"I wish I could meet up with this Jem," he said grimly.

"No need to feel sorry for me." She tilted her chin. "Nothing catastrophic happened. He's such a maggot. He just had all these urges. Men are like that."

"Indeed they're not," he rapped back. "Evil men give the rest of us ordinary decent guys a bad name. It's utterly unfair. There's something utterly disgusting about a predator."

"That's why I like my gay friends," she announced, wiping her hands daintily on a paper napkin before brushing back the damp curls at her temple.

"How long was your hair?" he asked, his eyes following the movement of her small, pretty hands.

"That's a funny question, Daniel Carson."

He gave his dimpled, lopsided smile. "Oh, I dunno. I'm trying to visualise you as the girl you were."

"If you *must* know, I had a great mop of hair. A lot of people thought it was lovely. Say, those sandwiches were good. I think I must have been starving. I might even have another one of those little pastries. Oh, it's yours!" she observed belatedly.

"Take it," he urged. "You're the one paying."

"What?"

"Just a little joke," he said. "My shout this time."

"Which reminds me," she said in quite a different voice. "I want you up at the house."

His eyebrows shot up. "You can't mean living there?"

"I can mean and I do mean." She sat back, fiddling with her thumbs.

"Just forget about it," he answered flatly.

"Might I remind you, Daniel, I'm the boss. I want you about two steps up the hallway from me. I don't know you very well, but I'd find having a great big guy like you around—especially one with a Swiss Army knife—reassuring."

He frowned direly. "Sandra, your fears are groundless."

"Sez you!" she responded hotly, sitting up straight. "Do you know how many people get killed over money?"

"There could only be one in a million who don't finish up in jail," he told her in a stern voice.

"A few more than that filter through," she struck back.

He studied the flare-up of colour in her cheeks. "Listen, Ms Kingston, if you're under the impression your family would agree to that, you're very much mistaken. Both your uncle and your cousin would see me gone only neither of them can do my job. It was your *grandfather* who hired me. It was your grandfather who gave me so much authority. As you can imagine your uncle and your cousin bitterly resented that fact, even if they didn't want to take over the reins. After twelve months I'll have no alternative but to quit."

"You *won't* quit while I need you," she told him

imperiously. "And you *will* shift your gear up into the house, if you'd be so kind. I may have been only ten when we were kicked out but I do remember it was so big you needed a bus to get around it."

"Just leave it for the time being, won't you?" he asked in his most reasonable voice. "See how the family reacts."

"In that case, Daniel, you better be present," she said. "So where did you come from anyway? Are you a Territorian?"

"I am now, but I come from all over."

"You're worse than I am," she sighed. "Could you be a bit more specific?"

"Maybe not today."

She looked at him searchingly. "So what about a compromise? Where *precisely* did you learn to manage a cattle station. You're what?" Her blue eyes ranged over him.

"You want me to produce a birth certificate? I'm twenty-eight, okay?"

"Most overseers aren't off the ground by then," she observed, impressed.

"Then I must be the eighth wonder of the world. As it happened, I learned from the best. My mother and I lived like gypsies moving around Outback Queensland until we came to rest in the Channel Country when I was about eleven. A station owner there, a Harry Cunningham, offered her the job of housekeeper after his wife died and there we stayed until he died some years back. His daughter sold the station almost immediately after. Something that must have the old man still swivelling in his grave. But such is life!"

There were a hundred questions she wanted to ask, but the first was easy. "So where is your mother now?"

His handsome face instantly turned to granite. "I'm like you, Alexandra. I'm an orphan."

"I'm sorry." She saw clearly he had no more dealt with the loss of his mother than she had the loss of her father. *Orphans*. Hadn't her mother been lost to her the day she married that rich, worthless scumbag, Jem?

"Not as sorry as I am," he said.

"What happened to her?" She spoke as gently as she could, fearing she was about to be rebuffed.

"I think we'll just leave it," he said.

CHAPTER TWO

HE TOOK her on a journey that filled her with fascination. The landscape beneath them was so vast, so timeless in character Sandra found herself awestruck. The first hellish minutes, just as she expected, had been taken up with fighting down her fears. She would never be cured of them. Not just of helicopters. In a chopper one couldn't look out on a fixed wing, causing not only in her, but in many people the sickening sensation the aircraft might simply drop out of the sky. She feared *all* aircraft. She'd been battling that particular phobia since she was a child and the family Cessna had taken a nosedive into the McDonnell ranges, not far from Moondai, with her father strapped into the pilot's seat. That was the start of it.

He did it, Sandy. Your uncle Lloyd. He caused it to happen. He'd know how. He was always jealous of your father. He couldn't let him inherit.

Some words are scorched into the memory as

were some scenes, like her mother sobbing out accusations...

He did it, Sandy. He couldn't let your father inherit.

So where did that leave her, her grandfather's heiress, all these years later? No way was she sitting pretty. Just like her father she was a target. But unlike her trusting father she had learned the hard way to always be on red alert. It helped too to have backup. Small wonder she'd decided, very sensibly, to shift her overseer into the homestead for a time. Daniel Carson had an aura that made a woman feel safe. She suspected there was more than a hint of Sir Galahad about him. She even liked the way he stared down at her from his towering height, though occasionally it had made her feel like toppling backwards.

He was an excellent pilot. He was handling the helicopter with such confidence and skill she was actually approaching a state of euphoria, where she believed nothing bad could possibly happen. Phobias were only there to be licked! The ride was so *smooth!* She gave herself up fully to the pleasure and excitement of the flight.

The immensity, the primeval nature and the remoteness of the landscape, lit by the brilliance of a tropical sun left an indelible imprint on the mind. This was a land unchanged in aeons. It appeared far more splendid than she remembered as a child. Of course there was no better way to see it than from a helicopter with its three-dimensional visual effects.

She felt as free as a bird, wheeling, skimming, darting across the glorious cobalt sky.

Great inundated flood plains glittered below them. She stared out eagerly. Rivers extended wall to wall in numerous spectacular gorges. Such places were inaccessible in the Wet. They could only be seen as she was seeing them, from the air. A foaming white waterfall was coming up on the right. It crashed over the towering stone escarpment, throwing up a white haze like a great curtain. In contrast, the walls of the canyon glowed like a furnace, a throbbing orange-red streaked with bands of iridescent yellow and pink. Millions of litres of water were being delivered into the turbulent stream below, although the rains had abated some weeks back.

Gradually as the inundated land began to settle there would be an abundant harvest. The animals and the birds would begin to breed. Wildflowers would open out, going to work to form a prolific ground cover over the warm, receptive earth. All the varieties of palms and pandanus would put out new fronds. The golden and crimson grevilleas would bloom, the hibiscus and gardenia would spread their scent and colour across a background of lush greens. Mere words couldn't prepare a visitor to the Top End for the sight. Suddenly after years in the city, Sandra felt the tremendous pull of the great living Outback. The Outback had fashioned her. She had been happily content as a child. Maybe she could be again?

Beneath her mile after mile of lagoons filled to the brim with beautiful waterlilies swept by. She knew the species: the sacred lily of Buddha, the red lotus, the pink and the white and the cream, and the giant blue waterlily with flowers that grew a foot across. The master of the waterways was down there, too. One could never forget that. The powerful salt water crocodile. She shuddered at the very thought. Moondai in the Red Centre was a long way from the crocs though according to the magnificent aboriginal rock drawings on the station they had inhabited the fabled inland sea of prehistory.

Daniel turned his handsome head to smile at her with a real depth of pleasure in his eyes. She smiled back, both of them in perfect accord; both captive to the space, the vast distances, the sunlight and the colours, the incomparable beauty of nature. Here was the very spirit of the bush. The air was so *clear,* it was like liquid crystal. By now, Sandra was so enthralled she'd completely forgotten how initially she had wanted to turn back. She felt happily content to fly with Daniel, an almost telepathic communication between them. It struck her he was really her kind of person. One knew these things right away.

It dawned on her very gradually their air speed was slowing. Steamy heat was rising from the water-logged soil.

"Everything okay?" She turned to him, an alarmed croak in her voice.

His profile was set in stone. "We're losing power. Sit tight."

Instantly Sandra jerked back in her seat. Panic surged through her chest, near driving the breath from her lungs. All illusions of safety were abruptly shattered. Her worst nightmares appeared to be coming true. They were in trouble. Didn't trouble follow her around? The helicopter was losing power *and* altitude. She craned her head. Beneath them lay a forest of paperbarks with their slender trunks standing in who knows how many feet of water. At least she could swim. She thought of the crocs. Their bodies would provide a nice feed. Troubled though her life had been she felt a sharp nostalgia for it. She wanted a *future!*

Okay, time to pray. What was the point, a dissenting little voice said. Her most fervent prayers hadn't saved Nikki from a tragically early death. She would pray all the same. She couldn't afford to get on the wrong side of God. Maybe *her* time was up? Hers and Daniel Carson's. Maybe that was why he didn't feel like a stranger? They were going to die together.

She was suddenly indignant. There had been *enough* trouble in her life. She deserved a break. She couldn't submit to her fate without paying strict attention to their plight. Not that she could do anything, basically, but try to help Daniel spot a place to set the chopper down.

Sandra stared fixedly at the magnificent landscape beneath them that had abruptly turned hostile. Daniel would have no other option but to force land.

Tell him something he doesn't know.

But where? The vast terrain was covered in glittering swamps with a canopy of trees growing so close together if they were monkeys they could scamper across it. She even had a fevered thought if the worst came to the worst, they could bail out, land in the water then if they were lucky spring up a tree with a prehistoric monster snapping at their heels.

If there was one thing Daniel had learned it was to stay cool under pressure. Even immense pressure like this. They were a few kilometres into a big, flooded paperbark swamp. The manifold pressure had dropped off and he was losing power and RPM. Air speed was declining as well. He knew the girl was only too aware of it and the consequent danger, though he was so focused on what he was doing he dared not turn his head to look at her or even speak.

Seventy knots to sixty and bleeding off fast. No matter how he wished otherwise he had Alexandra Kingston with him. A girl whose father had been killed in a plane crash.

He couldn't lose another second. He used his radio to report a mayday, giving his bearings. What could be causing this failure? He scanned the control panel which was going haywire. Something was screwing the system. The helicopter was regularly serviced as a matter of course. Only he flew it. And Berne.

He stared down, the muscles of his face rigid. There were huge paperbarks all around them fringed on the outer perimeter by pandanus.

Fifty knots.

God almighty! Was this the way it was going to end? A life span limited to a few decades? What a bloody mess. Adrenaline kicked in, flushing through his system. He was a good pilot, wasn't he? A very good pilot. Now was not the time to be modest. He was *lucky* as well, which was almost as good. He had the girl with him and she deserved a life. They had to survive. He had to land the chopper safely even if he clipped the rotors which was a strong probability. He could sense the girl beside him was sitting rigid with fear, but she wasn't screaming. Thank God for that! Many would be yelling their heads off at this point, when they were on the brink of a crash. She was, in fact, pointing frantically to a pocket handkerchief-sized clearing at the same time he spotted it coming up.

He lined the chopper up. The clearing was shaped like a playing field with its boundaries set at one end by a stand of pandanus, at the other by four paperbarks, their foliage iridescent in the sunlight.

Hell he almost loved her. She was far from stupid and she had kept her head. He had to applaud that.

Okay. It was now or never!

The swamp was rising to meet them with crocs in it for sure. Didn't you just love them? He had to judge the tips of the branches of the trees by centimetres. He could feel the tremendous rush of adrenaline through his body, even the thrill of extreme danger. Paradoxically it gave him a weird feeling of excitement as well as fear; a buoyancy he had experienced before in tight situations.

Ten metres above the water, the surface was quivering and shimmering like a sea of sequins, then it churned into waves by the strong down draught. He couldn't run the chopper on in case the skids got hooked onto the arched root system of the trees. If that happened, the chopper would flip over. A rotor tip only had to clip those trees. He could hear a hissing sound clearly. The clearing seemed to be lit up, preternaturally brilliant. It could signal the end but he took it as a good omen. He hovered, shutting everything out of his mind but the need to set the machine down safely. The will to survive transcended fear…all the blades were at the same pitch…

That's it. Hold it still. Praise the Lord!

At the last moment, Sandra shut her eyes, her small hands clenched into fists. Death was always waiting in the wings. She didn't want to see it coming. If she was going to die she was going to die. There was not much anyone could do about fate. But if anyone could save the situation this guy might.

Sweat was pouring off her yet her blood was running ice. They could drop like a stone. The chopper would be hurled around like a piece of debris before it went up in flames… It only needed one false move.

Though she waited in limbo for the moment of impact and probable annihilation, the chopper seemed to come down in ultra slow motion as the rotor blades set up a whirlwind. The machine didn't *hit* the water, rather it seemed to Sandra's bemused mind it came down as lightly as a brolga on its tippy toes. She felt the skids sink and held her breath in case the probing skids got caught up in the trees' root systems and tossed the fragile aircraft around like a child's toy. Dread paralysed her limbs. This was a nightmare!

Only slowly, so slowly, the skids settled on the swamp bed.

She couldn't believe it!

Sandra's eyes flew open. The chopper was bobbing on the surface of the swamp, the body surrounded by streams of bubbles. There was a gurgle of water somewhere but they were stable.

Eureka!

The aircraft gave a groan that was almost human. Daniel killed the engine. The beating rotors, main and tail, gradually stopped their thundering.

All was still.

Sandra couldn't even turn to face him. Whole moments passed while her racing heartbeats slowed to normal. Then she turned to him whooping triumphantly, unaware her face was milk-white with shock. "Carson, you have to be the coolest cat on the planet!"

"Supernatural!" he agreed wryly, tasting blood on his bottom lip.

They hit an exultant high-five.

"Which reminds me, you idiot! You could have killed us."

"I look on it more as a truly great save." Daniel stared at the control panel. "The person I should really kill is whoever's been tinkering with the chopper."

"What are you saying?" She heard the shrill note in her voice.

"Nothing. Absolutely nothing." Daniel backed off, removing his earphones and unbuckling his seat belt. "I have to get out and take a look. You stay here."

The very idea made her break out in a sweat. "You didn't think I was just going to jump in? There must be crocs in there."

He shook his head almost casually. "The water around us isn't deep. It's already begun to subside. Nevertheless we could become waterlogged even supposing I can fix whatever problem we have. The good thing is we're not far out of Darwin. Air Rescue will scramble another chopper in no time. I'll send you back with them. You'll have to be winched up. I'll stay with the chopper until we can get it airborne."

"So who's going to pinch it around here?" She resorted to sarcasm, not wanting to let him out of her sight. "The crocs? And don't tell me they're not lurking out there in among the reeds because I happen to know differently. I was born in the Territory, remember?"

"The *desert,* sweetheart," he jeered, not even aware in the stress of the moment he had called her that. "The Red Centre is completely different to the Top End. Desert and tropics, both in the Territory. Moondai might as well be a million miles away from the crocs."

"And I couldn't be happier about that," she retorted. "But shouldn't you stay put? You could come to a grim and gruesome end. I think I'd hate that."

He merely shrugged. "You don't happen to know how to handle a rifle?" He sounded extremely doubtful.

Sandra snorted. "Do I ever! My dad taught me how to handle a gun. I'm sure I remember. It's like learning to ride a horse."

Daniel studied her in amazement. "He must have started you off early?"

"Because I wanted to *learn,*" she replied tartly. "Bernie could shoot. I had to be able to shoot too in case he planned a little accident. Grandpop used to think becoming a good shot was character building. So what do you want me to do?"

He frowned. "I'm going to make a full circuit of the chopper. It's a miracle we didn't sustain any damage to the main rotor. We're centimetres from the trees. What I want you to do, if you feel up to it, is cover me just in case we have a nosey visitor. Just don't shoot *me,* okay? Want to have a run through first?'

She unbuckled her belt and stood up though her legs were still wobbly. "Might be an idea. Where's the rifle?"

He moved to collect it from where it was stashed, broke it open to load it, snapped the action shut, then passed it to her. "Think you know what you're doing?"

"I'd prefer a dirty great cannon," she muttered, making her own checks and feeling it all coming back. "But I do know which end of this thing shoots." She swung up the rifle and took aim through the chopper's reinforced forward windshield. "If there really is a croc out there where do I shoot him? Right between the eyes? They've got tiny brains haven't they?"

"I've never had the pleasure of finding out. Just don't miss or it will come right after me."

"Then me." She slicked stray tendrils off her forehead. "I'm ready if you are."

"Then let's *do* it!' he said.

He plunged straight down into the water which only a week before would have been over his head. "Fuselage appears to be unscathed," he called to her eventually, his eyes scanning the waxed, glinting sides. "I want to check the shafts of the tail rotor. Keep your eyes peeled for ripples in the water."

"Struth, what's with you? Of course I will. We're

dinner otherwise. They're there. I know they're there."

"Yeah? Well I'm the guy in the water." Daniel moved about near soundlessly in the swamp stirring up the mud on the bed so the shining water turned dark and murky. Sandra followed him from one side of the helicopter to the other, her keen young eyes focused on the surface.

"Skids are in a web of roots and vegetation," he yelled to her. "That's the danger. They'll have to be cleared."

"I bet there are leeches in there?" Her voice was level, her face pale but resolute.

"Too right. The little buggers are stuck to my legs."

"Oh how vile! You can't *do* anything, can you?" she called.

His voice came back to her sounding perfectly in control. "I'm going to use my old faithful Swiss Army knife. I have to clear that vegetation. Just cover me."

She watched him plunge beneath the muddied waters coming up with coils of vines and gnarled roots that he tossed away across the swamp.

Only now could she smell the stomach-turning odour of mud and rotting vegetation. "Finish soon, Daniel," she begged him. Her whole body was vibrating with tension and the rifle felt very heavy.

"Doing my best!" he grunted and plunged again.

A brilliant sun burned down on the small clearing,

the paperbarks and pandanus standing all around like sentinels. Sandra had never felt so exposed in her life.

Hurry, hurry, Daniel.

She saw his sodden dark head decorated with trails of luminescent green slime emerge at the very moment she spotted thirty feet beyond him an arrowhead of ripples across the stagnant surface of the swamp. Then at the apex of the triangle nostrils and behind that twin blackish bulges about twenty-two to twenty-three centimetres apart.

Eyes, that glinted gold!

She was so panicked for a moment she felt she might pass out. It was coming at surprising speed for such a great cumbersome creature. It was *surging* towards the challenger in its territory ready to dismember it limb from limb and stash the feast for a week later.

Horror was as sharp as a drill. "Get out!" she yelled. "Daniel, get out. It's a croc."

His lean, muscular body shot out of the water, his strong arms lunging at the body of the helicopter towards the open cockpit, hauling himself up.

Sandra took aim down the sights of the handsome bolt action rifle which had been fitted with a small telescope to make distant targets appear closer. Her whole face was pinched tight with control while she waited for the *precise* moment the giant reptile's brain, situated midway between the eyes, would be dead centre in her range. God help them if the action jammed!

Now!

She held her nerve. Her finger that had been holding steady on the trigger, squeezed… The butt plate kicked back into her shoulder as the firing pin struck the rear end of the cartridge.

The noise was deafening in the torrid, preternatural quiet of the swamp.

"I've killed it. I think I've killed it." Her voice was ragged. There were runnels of sweat running down her face. "Did I?" she called to him for confirmation, "or did I just nick it?" Now the crisis was over she was shivering. "I should have had an M16."

"Sorry, they belong to the armed forces." Swamp water was streaming off him, as he stood within the chopper, his boots oozing mud. Leeches were feasting off him. "No worries, you got him all right," he assured her. "Didn't you see his yellow belly as he rolled?"

"Hell I'm good!" she congratulated herself. "I hope he's not just playing dead? Maybe he wants both of us to think so until it's time to make a leap into the cabin."

He shook his head. "What do you want, a tooth for a trophy? You got him, Sandra. Good and proper. I would never have guessed you could shoot so well. You turned into Annie Oakley right before my eyes."

She staggered away to sit down. "Who's Annie Oakley anyway? One of your girlfriends?"

He moved to the edge of the doorway, beginning to remove the brown and black leeches with the help of his Swiss Army knife. "Hell, Ms Kingston, none of my girlfriends can shoot like you. You could give a lot of guys lessons. Annie Oakley, for your information, was a famous American markswoman. Supposedly Buffalo Bill's girlfriend though I believe she married someone else."

"Maybe it was a sore point she could shoot better. Uugh!" she shuddered, watching him remove the bloodsuckers with no show of revulsion. "How's this for adventure? What are you going to do to top it?"

A lock of wet raven hair flopped over one eye. He tossed his head to dislodge it. "I could carry you on my shoulders across the swamp?"

"No thanks."

"Changed your mind about going back with me?"

She hugged herself, rocking back and forth. "What do you reckon went wrong?"

"Too early to say." One leg was clear.

"You seemed pretty sure it was tinkering before?"

He kept silent, concentrating on the sickening task to hand.

"Do you mind answering?"

"Maybe I was a little too quick off the mark back there. The chopper will be checked out. Accidents happen all the time."

"There's nothing Uncle Lloyd and Bernie would like more than to see me dead," she said.

And I'd be a bonus, Daniel thought.

CHAPTER THREE

SANDRA awoke with a start. She ached all over. That's what happened when you had to be winched into a helicopter. She rolled over onto her back, throwing an arm across her eyes. She was in a hotel room back in Darwin, waiting for Daniel to make a reappearance. He had remained with Moondai's downed chopper while Air Rescue had ferried her back to Darwin. She really ought to get up, take a shower, tidy herself up. Everyone had been very kind to her, smoothing her way. She knew people would have been just the same had she not been Rigby Kingston's heiress.

It was night outside. Darwin throbbed with life but inside the hotel room all was quiet save for the hum of the airconditioning. It was a very nice room; thickly carpeted, nicely furnished, the decor suited to the tropical environment, softly lit, a beautiful big waterlily print behind the bed. She slid her bare feet to the floor, sat a moment, then walked over to the corner window looking out. Floors below her, the city was all lit up. A big yellow bus crawled along the main street, taxis whizzed up and down, a couple was turning into the hotel's entrance. Pedestrians crossed at the lights.

Where was Daniel? He seemed to stand alone as an ally. Their shared ordeal had established quite a bond, as such hair-raising incidents tend to do, although she'd been feeling quite kindly disposed towards him even before that. She knew he viewed her as a young person who needed looking after. A loner. An orphan. He seemed to identify with that. Her lack of height—she was five-two—had never helped. Actually she was very good at fending for herself. A result of having a mother like Pam who really loved her but somehow had never been able to demonstrate it as a parent should. Not that her mother hadn't had her own harrowing time. Losing her husband the way she had, then being thrown out of Moondai had caused huge psychological trauma.

Her ever present memories began flashing through her brain again. She let them roll like a video clip. There was her mother lying on a bed, an arm thrown across her swollen, tear-streaked face. There was she, a bewildered, grief-stricken child, standing beside the bed, her hand on her mother's shaking shoulder, trying to make sense of a world that had been turned violently upside down.

I loved your father, Sandy. Our marriage would

have survived if only he'd come away with me from Moondai. Moondai killed him. Moondai and your uncle Lloyd.

Uncle Lloyd said I'm not Daddy's. Is it true?

Would our marriage have survived if you weren't? Of course you're Daddy's little girl. Your uncle would say anything—anything at all—to try to discredit me.

Then how come Grandad threw us out? How could he do that if I'm his granddaughter?

Her mother's answer was always the same. *His grief was too powerful, Sandy. In a way he started to believe your uncle. But never, never doubt. You are Daddy's daughter. I swear to you on my life and his memory.*

Well, her doubts had persisted. It was only years later she had learned to thrust them aside. That was after her mother had married Jem—the second guy didn't count. Then she was truly on her own. She had never let her mother know what a sicko Jem really was. Her mother seemed happy with a man who liked to impose his will on everyone else, and now they had their son, her stepbrother, Michael, whom they both adored. Didn't she love Michael herself? Spoilt rotten Michael, despite the bad parenting was a nice little kid. And she was now an heiress who could have anything she liked. That's if she managed to survive the next six months. She would officially inherit on her twenty-first birthday in August. Her mother had interpreted that as Rigby Kingston trying to buy redemption.

How could her grandfather buy redemption when he hadn't had a soul?

Twenty minutes later she was showered, shampooed and dressed to descend to the hotel restaurant. She had scrubbed up rather nicely she thought, splashing out on makeup, a pretty dress, and a couple of squirts of perfume to give Daniel Carson a bit of a jolt. She was a *woman,* not the coltish youngster he thought he had taken under his wing. That attitude had set her a challenge and she liked challenges. She liked Daniel. He had saved her life. How could she not?

So where was he? Surely he'd be back by now, whether they'd been able to restart the helicopter or not. One thing was certain, a team of sharpshooters couldn't stick around in that swamp at night. It was crawling with crocs. A mechanic with the rescue team had been winched down to him. Maybe together they could get the chopper back in the air as they hadn't run out of fuel. It had to be some mechanical defect.

The digital clock said 7:23 p.m. She was hungry. All she'd really had all day was hers and Daniel's sandwiches and a cup of coffee. She was starting to worry about him. She didn't want to go ahead and eat without him. Even as she thought it, the phone rang. She reached it at speed.

"Ms Kingston?"

Mysteriously her heart leapt. Was that significant? "Daniel, where are you?" She hoped she didn't sound too needy. She wanted to project the weight of maturity.

"Keep calm. I'm down the hallway. Isn't that what you wanted? Your overseer close by."

"You bet. What happened about the chopper? Did you get it out?"

"It took a lot longer than expected. It's grounded for a complete inspection."

"So what was the problem?" She caught her reflection in the mirror, all pink cheeked and bright-eyed as if they were having a cosy chat.

"You wouldn't know if I told you."

"Just tell me this. Should we contact the police?"

"No way," he said.

He had such a sexy voice on the phone. It was sort of like being *caressed*. She took a deep breath. "Listen, we can't talk on the phone. I'm hungry."

"Aaah, yes, I remember your appetite. Give me ten minutes okay?"

She'd probably have given him an hour.

She was *full* of surprises Daniel thought in some amazement. So much for the immature, just-out-of-school girl without a scrap of makeup! What he saw in front of him was a dead sexy little buttercup blonde of at least twenty. She was wearing a swishy blue dress that doubled the impact of her violet eyes. Even her hair seemed to have trebled in height and thickness. For a few crucial moments he couldn't take his eyes off her. He damned well hadn't expected this transformation. Even her delicate breasts had perked up an inch or two. He was so astounded he had trouble hiding it, which didn't gel with his usual cool.

"Well good evening." He tried to smile his way out of it.

"Have a problem with the way I look, Daniel?" she asked sweetly, pleased at his readable reaction. Maybe she wouldn't take her little blue dress off.

"No, ma'am." He half shrugged. "You look different that's all.'

"*You* don't." She surrendered to the impish urge to put him in his place.

He winced. "So, you don't want to be seen with me?"

"I was only being a smart alec," she confessed, kindly.

He glanced down at himself. "I did try to order a dinner suit but they didn't have one in stock. I had to make do with what I've got on."

She made a business of looking him up and down as a prospective employer might the new chauffeur. What, she wondered, wouldn't he look good in? He was wearing what was obviously a new open necked shirt, white with fine beige and blue stripes and new denim jeans. "And those ridiculous boots?" she said, staring down at his feet. "You're towering over me."

"Yeah, well, most guys would. What was I supposed to do, buy a pair of loafers? This lot cost enough. My gear was ruined by the time we were finished in the swamp."

"Lose no sleep," she said loftily. "You'll be properly reimbursed."

"Thank you, ma'am." He bowed slightly.

"And you needn't be cheeky."

"I didn't know I was. I thought I was being respectful as befitting my position."

"Now that sounded sarcastic, Daniel," she warned, looking back over her shoulder for her clutch. "Where are we going?"

"Somewhere cheap," he said.

"*I'm* paying."

"That's different," he smiled, the dimple deep in his cheek. "I hope it suits but I've already made a booking at a little Vietnamese restaurant a short walk from here. I know the owners. The food's great."

"It's not noisy is it?"

"Not so it'll damage your ears." He studied the small face that had within a few short hours blossomed from a furled bud into full flower. "What's the problem, a headache?"

"I'm sick with nerves, Daniel, if you must know." She walked back to pick up her purse.

"I promise I'll lay down my life for you." He said it lightly with a grin. Then it struck him. He had just said something he actually *meant*.

She paused in front of him, wide-eyed. "Promise?"

Daniel felt the need to swallow. "No one will so much as tweak a hair of your head," he said, trying to fight out of a daze.

"My hero!"

If he weren't shocked enough, she upped the ante by going on tiptoes and landing a kiss on the point of his jaw.

The food was as good as he had promised and more. The restaurant was small but fully booked. Only Daniel was clearly a favourite they would regrettably have been turned away.

"How come everyone likes you?" Sandra asked, tucking into prawns in a delicious spicy sauce.

"It's my sunny nature," Daniel explained. "*Not* everyone likes me, however. My boyish charm doesn't work on your uncle Lloyd or Berne. Berne and I often have words."

"What about?" she asked with interest.

He shrugged. "Just about anything sets Berne off."

"So he hasn't changed," she said dryly.

"I never had the great pleasure of knowing him when he was a kid."

"He was the biggest pain in the arse in all the world. Pardon the language." She glanced around hoping no one had heard her. Mercifully they were all too busy eating.

"You obviously feel strongly," he remarked, underlining the *strongly*.

"I apologised, didn't I? So, did you find anything suspicious? You can tell me now."

"Nothing we could pin on anyone." He shrugged. "If you really want to know it was like this." He launched into a detailed account of their preliminary findings until she held up her hand.

"Sorry. Like they say, that's way over my head. The real question is, are you game to charter another chopper and fly back to Moondai? More to the point, am I game to go with you?"

"It's the only way I know to get there, unless we walk." He forked another sea scallop.

"Do I need to remind you I'm an heiress?"

"No, ma'am."

"You're not going to keep calling me ma'am are you?" she asked crossly.

"I thought as you're my boss, I should. You don't seem to like Ms Kingston."

"What if dear old Uncle Lloyd is right and I'm *not* a Kingston?" she asked waspishly, then resumed eating.

"You must be. You remind me of your grandfather."

That set her beautiful eyes asparkle. "Do you want to hold on to your job, Daniel?"

"I've got nothing better at the moment," he said, calmly returning her stare.

A fraught moment passed. "Tell me about your-self," she invited, seemingly able to assume a cajoling voice at will. *"Please."*

"You really want to know?"

"Would I have asked if I didn't? To be honest, after surviving today's little mishap I feel we're meant to be friends." To prove it she solemnly took a scallop from his plate.

"Then I wouldn't lay it on you."

"That bad?"

Relaxed and smiling a minute before, he suddenly looked grim. "Absolutely awful. Your own child-hood couldn't have been a dream?"

"It was okay until we lost Dad. Then everything changed. He used to call out from the front verandah, "Hi, my little darlin', I'm home." It wasn't my mother he was talking to. It was me. Sometimes I think both my parents needed their heads examined getting hitched."

He nodded. "Another case of if only I knew then what I know now. It makes me very wary of having a passionate affair."

"Now that I can't swallow." She threw him a look of disbelief.

"Meaning what?"

She shrugged a delicate shoulder. "I imagine there's no end of women willing to go orgasmic— is there such a word?—over you."

"Sandra, for that you need a good spanking."

"Please," she moaned. "Don't you dare talk down to me."

"I didn't mean to." Frankly he was at a complete loss how to treat her. It was easier before when she looked like a little damsel in distress, but now? Just looking at her made him gulp for air.

"That's okay then." She nodded briskly. "I'm twenty, soon to be twenty-one. I've led an adventurous life. Some might say *seedy*. I think *I* would in my place."

His tongue got the better of him. "So why am I convinced you're a virgin?" As soon as he said it he could have bitten his tongue out because street smart as she claimed to be she coloured up furiously.

"Daniel Carson our relationship does *not* extend to discussing subjects like that." She tilted her head, looking down her small perfect nose. "What do you mean anyway? When I had all my hair and I was six kilos heavier I was *hot!*"

He couldn't help himself. He laughed aloud. "You'd set off a few smoke alarms right now." He hadn't missed the appreciative glances coming her way especially from one guy who might need sorting out. "Better get cracking then and put back those six kilos. Would you like to consult the menu again?" he asked helpfully.

"Are you having a go at me?" Her expression was sharp.

"Would I dare?" He raised his black brows.

"There's actually nothing I like better than to see a girl with a healthy appetite."

She shrugged. "Maybe dining with you wasn't a good idea. All I've had all day was those sandwiches at the airport. Besides I can afford it remember? I'm an heiress. Except I don't want to be and I don't want Moondai."

"I think you can be persuaded to change your mind. Moondai is a wonderful place."

"Well it makes *your* eyes light up," she commented. "*You're* not hoping to marry me, are you?" She cocked her head to one side. "Because I have to tell you I'm not an easy target. Being an heiress attracts scores of guys."

"I wouldn't be a bit surprised if you finished up with several hundred suitors," he retorted, watching the waiter approach with their main course, chilli baked reef fish.

"Daniel Carson, you're *priceless!*"

"No, I'm one of those guys who like to make their own way in life, Alexandra."

"You'd better point out another if you see one," she returned breezily. "Oh goody, here comes the waiter! What about dessert?"

"You can have dessert if you want," he replied. "They do a delicious coconut dish with gula melaka syrup and another ginger one that's very good. I'm going to have one."

"How could they ever fill you?" She was in awe of his height and superb physique.

"My sweet little mother used to say that to me nearly every day of the week. *How am I going to fill you, Danny?*"

Some tender note in his voice, the poignant expression on his dynamic face tugged on her heart strings and made her close her eyes.

"Hey what are you doing?" he asked in alarm as a teardrop ran from beneath her thick lashes and down her cheek. "Sandra?"

She opened her eyes and choked back a cough. "Something went down the wrong way," she lied.

"Here, have a glass of water." He began to pour one.

"Thanks." She drank a little, looking up brightly as the Vietnamese waiter arrived at their table. "Ah, this looks sensational!" She smiled.

He was out of it—after all it had been quite a day—when the insistent ring of the phone ripped him out of the enveloping clouds.

"Daniel? Get down here fast," a voice hissed.

Instantly he was on red alert. "Sandra?"

"Someone else you know?" she asked sharply. "There's some guy at my door. He keeps tapping and asking, 'Are you in there, blondie?'"

"I'm on my way." Daniel was already pulling on his jeans. This was just the sort of thing the attractive blond women of this world had to put up with, he thought wrathfully. He shouldered into his shirt, not bothering to button it. Sandra was several rooms along from him down the corridor. He was at the very end of the hallway.

Outside in the passageway, he caught the back of a heavily built guy, not tall, striding purposefully towards the lift. At that hour—it was 2:30 a.m.—there was no one else about. Daniel recognised him immediately as the guy in the restaurant who'd been giving Sandra looks Daniel hadn't cared for. "Hey," he called, lengthening his own stride. "Hold it there, fella!"

"You talkin' to me?" The man swung round, on his face an expression of challenge.

"You see anyone else nipping around at this hour?" Daniel closed the distance between them. "You staying at this hotel?"

"Sure I am," the guy blustered.

"Name and room number, please?"

"You security or somethin'?"

Daniel was reminded of a cornered bull. "Right on," he clipped off, daring the other man to question him further. "I've just had a phone call from a hotel guest saying some idiot was tapping on her door, wanting an invite in. Could that possibly be you?"

The guy swore. "Look I'm lost, okay? Had a bit too much to drink with a couple of my mates. Probably on the wrong floor."

"So what's your room number, Mr.?" Daniel

pressed his body forward slightly so the other guy had to back up.

"Three Fourteen and it's Rick Bryce."

"Well I agree with you when you say you've had too much to drink and you *are* on the wrong floor."

"Listen, mate." The guy started his appeal. "I don't want any trouble."

"Then you won't mind if I escort you to your room? Management might have a couple of quick questions."

Minutes later when Daniel tapped on Sandra's door, softly calling her name, she opened it a fraction peering at him with huge eyes.

"Come in." She made a grab for his shirt, trying ineffectually to pull him through the door.

"We're going to have a conversation then?" He made it easy by stepping inside. She was wearing what looked like a flirty mini but was probably the latest in nightwear. Her small face was distressed. He knew distress on a woman's face when he saw it.

"Was *he* the guy?" she asked. "I peeped out and saw you talking to him. You had him backed right up against the wall like you were going to give him a good biff."

"He won't be bothering you again. Count on it."

"Is he staying in the hotel?"

Daniel nodded. "Several floors down. His name is Rick Bryce. He claims he had a bit too much to drink and got mixed up with the floor."

"Rubbish!" she said fiercely, shaking her head. "Why does this stuff happen to me?" she moaned, crossing her arms over her delicate breasts.

"What stuff?" He watched her suddenly take off on a rage around the room.

"Men knocking on my door." She threw her arms wide. "Men trying to get in. Stop asking me questions."

"Sandra, settle down," he said soothingly. "You don't have anything to worry about. I promise."

She exhaled noisily. "I felt like he could break in. I knew he couldn't, but I felt he could." Her eyes were swallowing up her face.

"You should have rung management immediately." He looked back at her intently. Suddenly remembering the things she had told him, the little pieces started to fall into place.

"I rang *you* didn't I?" she cried. "I knew you'd be here in a few seconds. I trust you, Daniel. I don't trust anyone else."

"Gee that's sad," he said quietly, running a hand through his sleep-tousled hair. "So, are you going to go back to bed? We have a big day tomorrow."

"Sure." She looked sheepish all of a sudden and a tad ashamed. "Thanks a lot, Daniel. Sorry I had to wake you up."

"That's absolutely no problem at all. You're certain you're okay?" She looked very pale and agitated.

"He gave me a fright, that's all. Don't you ever get a fright?" She turned roundly on him.

"So what's this really about?" he asked, his voice quiet and reassuring. "The odious stepfather?"

Colour swept her pale cheeks. "Don't be so stupid, Daniel," she raged. "I've been over that for years." She swung away from him, her exposed nape, her delicate shoulders and the fine bones of her shoulder blades like little wings so vulnerable to his eyes. The fabric of her nightdress was gossamer light. For a little space of time he could see through it as she moved into the glow of the bedside lamps. The outline of her young body was incredibly erotic. Emotions assailed him, very real and very deep but he thrust them vigorously away. He was her knight in shining armour wasn't he?

"That's a *yes*, Daniel," she burst out, turning back to him. There was a little vein beating frantically at the delta of her throat. "I hated...I *hated*..."

Images sprang to Daniel's mind that gave him a chill. "He must have been a real sick, sad bastard, your stepfather. I'd like to meet up with him. As for your mother!" His face was dark with disgust.

"Leave her out of it, okay?" she said fiercely. "She did her best."

"Some best!" Daniel threw himself down into an armchair. "Do you want me to wait here until you fall off to sleep?"

Her beautiful eyes quieted. A passing ripple of expression told him she liked the sound of that, but she looked at him coolly, the twenty-year-old with attitude. "Kinda kooky isn't it, Carson?" she challenged.

"Not at all." He shrugged, lifting his arms and locking them behind his head. "You're not all grown-up until you're twenty-one. Why don't you just hop into bed and close your eyes. I promise I won't leave until you're fast asleep."

"Can we talk for a bit?" She slipped beneath the coverlet, her body so ethereal a man would have to shake the sheets to find her.

"No," he said firmly. "Plenty of time to talk tomorrow. Close your eyes now."

She sat up briefly. "Will you tell me something, Daniel?"

"If I can." Sometimes she sounded so darn endearing.

"Wouldn't you have liked a younger sister?"

He thought of his early life the way it was. No place for a little sister. "There was only room for me and my mum."

"You'd have made a lovely brother, too." She sank back again, sounding young and wistful.

"*Good night*, Sandra," he said pointedly.

"All right, all right." She plumped up the pillow, irritable again, then punched it. "By the way, thanks. Did I say thanks?"

"Yes, you did."

"One more request. Do you think I can have a glass of water?"

"Okay." He stood up, wondering briefly and wildly what it might be like to join her. "After that, you promise to be good?"

"I promise." She gave him an utterly beautiful smile.

He walked into the ensuite, filled one of the glasses with water, then returned to the bedside. "Here." He put the glass into her hand.

She took a couple of quick gulps then passed the glass back to him. "I'm so glad you were here tonight. You're really dedicated to your work, aren't you, Daniel?" She stared up at him as though he just might give her a brotherly peck on the forehead.

Instead he gave her a quick glance with silver eyes cool. "Yes, ma'am." He put the glass down on the bedside table, then turned off the lamps, leaving one burning in the ensuite. He moved well away from the bed, resuming his seat in the armchair. Once there, he threw back his head and started to snore.

"It's all right, Daniel. I've got the message." She giggled softly at the sounds he was making, snuggled up to the pillow and closed her eyes.

"Don't worry about a thing," he murmured, letting his own eyelids drop. "I'm here."

CHAPTER FOUR

IN THE end Daniel was able to get them aboard a nine seater charter flight bound for the Alice. The station helicopter remained grounded in Darwin undergoing a more thorough inspection than the one hurriedly carried out at the swamp site. All Sandra knew was it had something to do with mechanical components in the tail rotor that had worked their way loose.

It was almost noon before the twin engine Cessna landed on Moondai, depositing them on the station strip before taking off on the last leg of the flight into Alice Springs. The Alice as it is affectionately known is located almost in the very centre of the continent and the town that most symbolises the legendary Red Centre. Sandra had memories of going with the family to the annual fun carnivals the town put on. There was the annual Henley-on-Todd regatta when teams raced in leg-propelled, bottomless boats across the dry bed of the ancient river.

Everyone, locals and tourists alike, delighted in the ridiculousness of it all. Then there was the Alice Springs annual rodeo with big prize money. Her father had often competed in that. But the festival she had most loved as a child was the riotous Camel Cup Carnival also raced in the dry bed of the Todd River. Those memories, mostly fond, reassured her if only slightly. She was extremely nervous of meeting up with her dysfunctional family again. Why wouldn't she be? Her grandfather's will had left her immeasurably better off than them.

She looked around this remote world that was now hers. She had almost forgotten the size of the place, the primal *stillness* like a great beast sleeping. The fiery colours of the earth contrasted wonderfully with the deep cloudless blue of the sky. "What, no welcoming party?" she quipped.

"Amazingly, no." Daniel picked up her luggage and piled it into the back of a station Jeep that was parked with the keys in it. "Did you want one?"

"It's all too late for that, Daniel," she sighed with resignation. "You know and I know they hate me."

"Win them over," he advised.

"Don't joke, I'm *serious*."

"So am I. Just give yourself *and* them a chance."

"Right!" She pulled a face. "I'll have them eating out of my hand."

"Like me," he said, dryly.

She felt a flush of heat run right through her body.

That had sounded so *nice!* "So what do you suppose Grandpop was thinking when he left the lion's share to me?" she asked, trying to act cool.

"Reparation?"

"Maybe." She raked her fingers through her cropped hair. "What's the worst they can do to me, do you reckon? Carry on bitterly resenting me, or move right on to hatching *more* plans to get rid of me? And *you,* for that matter. I can't wait until we get the final report on the chopper. It seemed very convenient to get downed in a crocodile infested swamp. I mean tiny ole me mightn't have made much of a meal, but *you* surely would have."

"Well it didn't happen. You turned into Annie Oakley right before my eyes. Anyway, you can bet your life there'll be nothing to *prove.* The chopper held up for the flight from Moondai to Darwin. Anyway there's no point in speculating. Let's wait and see. Don't be afraid."

"It takes courage to act unafraid," she said quietly.

"You've got it," he said. She had proved that at the swamp.

"How can you say that after what happened last night?" She frowned into the shimmering distance. The desert mirage was at play creating its fascinating illusions. Today it was long ribbons of lakes with vigorous little stick people having a corroboree around the shores.

"Hey, don't look so worried." His tone was light.

"*What* happened exactly? I stayed with you until you fell asleep which was almost immediately. I'm not so insensitive that I can't understand what living with that stepfather of yours did to you. Besides you're not alone in your fears of being on your own in a hotel room with some drunken oaf pestering you. It would upset most women."

"You think he'll do it to someone else?"

Daniel opened the passenger door for her. "I've had a word with a couple of people and they in turn will have a word with others connected to the hotel business. They'll be on the lookout for him."

"He kept calling me *blondie!*" Sandra took her seat in the station vehicle.

"Forget it. It's over." Daniel climbed behind the wheel beside her, turning the ignition.

"Stay by me, Daniel," she urged.

The drive up to the homestead seemed to go on forever. She'd forgotten about all the *space!* They passed numerous outbuildings which all looked solid and cared for, painted a pristine white. Colourful desert gardens thrived around the married staff's bungalows and the bunk houses for the single men. It all presented with so much character and appeal it could have been the setting for some Western movie.

"Someone is doing a good job around here," Sandra said with approval as they approached the walled home compound.

"Thank you, ma'am." Daniel took credit where it was due. "It makes me happy to hear you say that."

"It'd make me a lot happier if you wouldn't call me ma'am."

He gave her an ironic glance. "Don't take it personally. I'll call you Sandra when we're on our own. In front of your family and the staff I'd like to leave it as ma'am or Ms Kingston. Take your pick. Think about it, Sandra. It's more respectful and it will make for fewer waves. I couldn't imagine taking liberties with your grandfather and calling him Rigby. He was always Mr. Kingston."

"He was more than seventy!" Sandra pointed out scornfully.

"Well until you're approaching seventy I think I'd better stick to calling you Ms Kingston."

"How would you like it if I called you *Mr. Carson?* For that matter are you sure Daniel mightn't be considered too familiar?"

He shook his head. "No, Daniel's okay. Your grandfather called me Dan. I should tell you now what you would have learned had you paid attention to the reading of the will. Your grandfather left me $250,000 on top of my normal salary providing I stayed on for a period of twelve months."

Her mouth fell open in astonishment. "Was that the *only* way he could get you to stay?"

"You don't think I might have earned it?" He glanced at her with glinting eyes.

"Now that's a stupid question. I'm *sure* he made you earn it. It's just so unexpected. Did Grandpop find his heart at the last minute or was he counting on *you* to prop *me* up?"

"Absolutely!" His voice sounded amused. "That's until you make a decision, Ms Kingston."

She swung her head. "I don't see anyone in the back seat."

"A little practice will make Ms Kingston come easier," he told her reasonably. "I might have been in your grandfather's good books, but that's where it stopped. Lloyd and Berne bitterly resented my influence with him. Berne went ballistic when he heard about my legacy."

"When it had nothing to do with him," Sandra said crisply. "They got plenty. They can stay in the house for as long as they like."

"That will make it hard all round."

"You bet!" she said drolly.

They were driving through an avenue of venerable old date palms with massive trunks. It was all coming back to her. Beyond the eight foot high wall smothered in a bright orange bougainvillea she would get her first glimpse of the homestead from which she and her mother had been banished. At least the tall iron gates were wide open in some sort of welcome, launching them into the home gardens.

The light dazzled. The wind caught boldly coloured blossom and sent it whirling to the ground.

Native trees soared, all manner of eucalypts, acacias, casuarinas, a few exotics that had survived the dry conditions, clusters of the beautiful ghost gums she loved, underplantings galore, jasmine clamouring everywhere scenting the air.

This is all mine!

She spoke aloud in wonderment. "Can you believe it? I own all this."

"Lucky you!" Daniel said, giving her a sardonic look. From apprehension she had gone to excitement. The big question would be, did this place speak to her? Had she really come home or would she stay a while then put it on the market? He'd had experience of that. He knew had he been born to a splendid inheritance he would have used every skill he possessed to build it up further and hold it for his heirs. But fate was a fickle thing. Rigby Kingston had amassed wealth and a pivotal role serving his country as a big beef producer. He had lost the one son who might have been able to assume his father's mantle but neither his remaining son nor his grandson had what it took to be a cattleman or to even play a significant role in the running of the station. How could Moondai fare better with a young woman at the helm? The cattle business had always been a male-orientated concern for obvious reasons. It was a hard life, too tough for a lone woman. Had Rigby Kingston mapped out a plan he hoped might work?

The Kingston heiress was addressing a question to him, bringing him out of his speculations. "Just what do Uncle Lloyd and Berne do with themselves all day? They surely can't sit around the homestead?"

"Your uncle has his all consuming interest, botany."

"Still at it, is he?"

"I understand his knowledge of the native flora is encyclopaedic. No small thing. Berne works around the station. Nothing too stressful."

"That must make it difficult for both of you as you're not friends?"

"Not even remotely," he assured her, "but I try to give him space. Your uncle involves himself in the business side of things from time to time, though Andy Fallon—he's an accountant and a good one—runs the office. Do you remember him?"

Sandra shook her head. "He must have arrived after we left. What about Elsa? She might have been Grandad's second wife, but Mum always called her *The Ghost!*"

"Well she does move around the place very quietly," Daniel said, thinking that was pretty well the way he too pictured Elsa. "She bothers no one." Daniel was still wondering how Rigby Kingston had ever married such a socially inept woman, especially after the idolized first wife, Catherine, who had died fairly early of cancer. "Lloyd and Berne hardly acknowledge her, which is pretty sad. Meg is still the housekeeper. You must remember Meg?"

"Of course! Meg stood on the front verandah tears pouring down her face as we were being driven away. She was always very kind to me, looking after me when Mum was away on her city jaunts."

Is that what Pamela had called them, Daniel thought cynically. City *jaunts?* He had heard so much about Pamela he now felt a lot of the bad stuff had to be true.

"We're almost here," he said, casting her another quick glance. In the baking heat she looked as fresh as a daisy, her skin as smooth and poreless as a baby's. She wore a neat little top almost the same colour as her hair and navy cotton jeans that were chopped off midcalf. The feisty look on her face, the angle of her small, delicately determined chin, were only self protection. He knew she was thrumming with nerves.

And he was right. Sandra stood out on the broad paved circular driveway looking up at the house that had figured so frequently in her dreams. Now she was the *owner,* about to inspect the premises and renew her troubled relationship with her family. Not that she had ever considered Elsa, *family,* which was really odd given Elsa's status. But Elsa had never involved herself, standing curiously aloof from them all. Her mother was right. Elsa had acted more like a visitor than mistress of Moondai. Strange behaviour from a woman who at one stage had run an Outback charter company with her first husband, a confirmed womaniser. Pamela always said divorce from that first philandering husband had dealt a blow to Elsa's psyche from which she had never recovered.

"So what do we do now?" Daniel looked to her for further instructions.

"You come up with me," Sandra said. "Every girl needs a Daniel when she's walking into the lion's den."

Moondai homestead was built of beautiful golden limestone, arcaded on both levels, the ground floor open, the upper level bordered by white wrought-iron balustrading. Tall, graceful vertical French doors set off the horizontal mass of the impressive façade. The shutters to the French doors were and always had been painted a subtle ochre to complement the golden limestone. The entrance hall was guarded by beautifully carved tall double doors with brass fittings that gleamed from many years of frequent polishing.

As Sandra peered into the cool interior a tallish, thin figure suddenly appeared, ankle-length skirt flapping, as if caught in a draught.

"It's Elsa, Sandra," Daniel prompted, in case there was any confusion. Elsa Kingston had aged a great deal even in the time he had been on Moondai.

"Gawd!" Sandra breathed irreverently. This wasn't the Elsa she remembered. Elsa had been a handsome blonde woman showing her German heritage in her bone structure and colouring. Not only had she aged she'd lost stones in weight.

Elsa approached, holding out her arms. "Alexandra! Welcome home, my dear."

Sandra responded at once. "Forgive me, Elsa, I didn't recognize you for a moment."

"I dare say I've changed a lot." Elsa not only hugged her, but she kissed Sandra on both cheeks.

"I suppose *I* have, too," Sandra answered tactfully, dismayed by Elsa's appearance and trying hard not to show it. "Thank you for the welcome." As a child Elsa had never ever so much as patted her on the head. Why now the affectionate greeting, even if she was grateful for it?

"Let me look at you!" Elsa stood back, staring at Sandra with eyes that had faded from their clear, striking light blue to almost colourless. Her once fine-grained skin was a maze of wrinkles. Clearly she hadn't cared for it in the Outback sun. Her long thick blonde hair, once her best feature, she had allowed to turn a yellowish-grey. Today it was bundled into a thick knot with stray locks flying loose. She wore no makeup to brighten her appearance. Her clothes could have been bought at a Thai street stall. The whole effect was one of eccentricity. Sandra felt a deep stirring of pity. This shouldn't *be!* Elsa looked as if the life had been drained out of her.

"You're still the image of your mother," Elsa was

saying, "though you're so thin. I can't catch even a glimpse of your poor father."

"Nevertheless his blood runs through my veins," Sandra said, determined not to become upset. "Daniel will be staying in the house for a while, Elsa. I intend to learn as much as I can about the operation of Moondai in the shortest possible time. I want my manager on hand."

Elsa didn't look like she was about to argue. "Just as you say, dear." She nodded. "It's a very big house. There's plenty of room. What about the west wing?"

"I'll look around first," Sandra said, softening it with a smile. The west wing was about as far away from the main bedrooms as one could get. She endeavoured to move forward, but Elsa seemed oblivious to the fact she was blocking the way. "Where's the rest of the family?" Sandra couldn't prevent the touch of sarcasm.

"They're waiting for you in the library," Elsa said in a voice that conveyed disapproval. "I should have asked immediately, forgive me, but how are you feeling after your scare? Lloyd told me about the mishap to the helicopter. Such dangerous things, helicopters. *All* light aircraft!"

"We survived, Elsa," Sandra answered dryly.

"Thank God," Elsa responded with what sounded like genuine fervour. "Do you *want* to stay at the house, Dan?" She turned to Daniel uncertainly.

"I'm here to do whatever Ms Kingston wants," Daniel replied in his courteous voice. "Mr. Kingston trusted me to carry out his orders."

"You weren't afraid of him, were you, Dan?"

Daniel looked unsurprised by the question or the bleakness of Elsa's tone. "I didn't see anything to *be* afraid of, Mrs. Kingston."

Elsa's gaze went beyond him, as if looking into the past. "He was a hard, *hard,* man. No heart, no compassion."

"He did live through a terrible tragedy," Daniel offered quietly.

"Where's Meg?" Sandra sought to break up the sombreness of the exchange. She looked about her. The black and white marble tiles of the entrance hall gleamed, the woodwork shone. A beautiful antique rosewood library table stood in the centre of the spacious hall, adorned by a large bronze urn filled with an arrangement of open and budded blue lotus with their seed pods and open and furled jade coloured leaves. Everything with the exception of Elsa looked *cared* for.

"She has a few more jobs to do, Alexandra," Elsa said. "You'll see her soon."

"Good. I'm looking forward to it. Probably at lunch. You want lunch don't you, Daniel?"

"A sandwich will do me fine." Daniel shrugged off lunch with the warring Kingstons. "Like Meg I have plenty of work to do."

"Shall we go through to the library?" Elsa asked, long thin hands fluttering like birds on the wing.

"Actually, Elsa, I'd like to freshen up first." Sandra lifted her head to the first floor gallery that was hung with pictures. "Which room have you given me?"

Elsa's gaze dropped as if to consult the marble tiles. "I thought your old room…perhaps you might want another…Meg said you should choose…I wasn't sure…"

"Thank you," Sandra said. "I'll look around before I decide." Her family had kept her waiting. Now they could wait for her. "You can bring up my luggage now, Daniel." She gave the order, mock lady of the manor.

"Yes, ma'am." There was an answering wicked light in Daniel's eyes but Elsa, still fixating on the tiles, didn't notice.

"So what have you in mind?" Daniel asked, after they had negotiated the divided staircase and were several feet along the east wing.

"Not the master suite that's for sure," Sandra said. "I bet Uncle Lloyd has moved in there already."

"I wouldn't know."

"Let's check it out!" Sandra rushed ahead. The hallway was still carpeted with the same valuable Persian runner.

She threw open her late grandfather's bedroom

door, gasping a little to see it was indeed occupied by her uncle. Books spilled everywhere. A pair of glossy riding boots stood near the massive bed and a magnificent silk dressing gown was thrown carelessly over a deep leather armchair. "Right! Uncle Lloyd in residence. I doubt very much if it's Bernie. I don't want it anyway. I'll have my parents' suite. *You* can have my old room, Daniel. That way you'll be near me."

"Does it have a dear little bed?" Daniel asked sarcastically, wondering how he could be remotely comfortable living up at the house let alone in what had been a small girl's bedroom.

She turned her head over her shoulder. "I trust you. You trust me. You can have any furniture you want, Daniel. Just don't interfere with my plans."

"Yes, ma'am."

"We're alone, aren't we?"

"Your ancestors are on the wall." He cast a glance at them.

"Arrogant looking bunch aren't they?"

"Don't mistake arrogance for iron determination," he said. "The Kingstons and others like them pioneered an industry. They pioneered what is still in many ways wild frontier country."

"I stand corrected, Daniel," she said, mock repentant. "Are you sure your dad wasn't a cattleman?"

His gaze had the cool intensity of a big cat's.

"Ms Kingston, I'm not sure *who* my dad was," he said bluntly.

The colour in her cheeks went from soft pink to crimson. She put out a tentative hand. "Daniel, I didn't mean to hurt you."

"You haven't," he assured her crisply. "Let's get you settled."

"Right." She surged forward. "It's along here." She pointed and Daniel followed with her case. "You're over there."

"God, Sandra. It's opposite yours."

She raised haughty brows. "So what's so disturbing about that? It's not as though we intend playing little seduction games."

"Indeed no!" he said sternly.

"Oh come off it, Daniel. I couldn't care less where you sleep as long as it's close by. You can get someone to help bring up your things."

"I'm not happy about this," Daniel said, shaking his head.

"And I understand. But, Daniel, I *need* you. I'm not asking you to move in with me so quit pulling those anxious faces. I'm like a soldier who needs backup in a combat zone. Think of it like that."

They found Lloyd Kingston and his son Bernard, sitting in splendour in the library—an *enormous* room—which housed thousands of books and maps which no one to Sandra's knowledge had ever read, or even attempted to read outside herself. As a child she had loved climbing up and down the moveable ladder, pulling out books on the adventures of the early explorers, crying over their deaths in the desert. Uncle Lloyd had always kept his huge collection of botanical books quite separate from the library. For one thing her grandfather, if he hadn't exactly ridiculed his son's consuming interest in plants, was extremely irritated and disappointed by Uncle Lloyd's lack of interest in the cattle business, or indeed business in general. Bernie too barely tolerated his father's passion for wildflowers, herbs, native plants and the like but he, no more than his father, had enjoyed station life. What they both enjoyed was reaping the benefit of Rigby Kingston's success. Finding "enlightenment" her grandfather had called it when her uncle Lloyd took off on his field trips.

So far it didn't look like he had found it. Though Rigby Kingston's will had left them both rich, neither Lloyd nor Bernie had made the slightest attempt to vacate the family home. Likewise Elsa who was still nipping at Sandra's heels wearing the long-suffering expression of an early Christian martyr.

"Sandra, my dear." Lloyd Kingston rose to his impressive feet, with quite an air of bonhomie. He came towards his niece as though he too, like Elsa, meant to catch her into a bear hug.

"Uncle Lloyd! You haven't changed a bit." Sandra suffered the hug which was mercifully brief. "You're as handsome as ever." As indeed he was. Tall, dark haired, eyes so dark they were almost black. He hadn't gained weight in midlife though his upper torso had thickened somewhat lending him more substance. Lloyd turned his head. "Berne, come greet your cousin." Narrowed eyes swept over the silent Daniel. "You may go now, Daniel." The politeness of the tone didn't conceal the order. "That was a terrible business with the helicopter. And so awful for Sandra! What exactly happened again? You did tell me when you called."

Daniel gave him a direct look. "It's being thoroughly checked over, Mr. Kingston. I prefer we wait on the full report. It might take time."

"You're the only guy I know who could have landed it." Berne Kingston moved to join the group, giving off an aura of aggression plain for all to see.

"Maybe someone wasn't counting on it," Sandra said. "How are you, Bernie?"

His mouth twisted but he made no attempt to touch her nor she him. "Long time no see." He examined Sandra carefully from head to head. "You're so like Aunty Pam it hurts," he said finally. "Except Pam would have made two of you. You've scarcely grown. And what's with the hair?"

"Nothing terminal," she answered, "so don't get your hopes up. I didn't expect to see you here,

Bernie. Were you waiting around especially to welcome me home?"

"You can't honestly believe that?" he asked flatly.

"I don't."

"You've one hell of a nerve. I'll say that for you." He gave a brief laugh. "Always did even as a kid. I don't know what Grandad was thinking of—he always was devious, but Moondai should have gone to Dad, not you, and me, before you. You were last in line."

"The last shall be first."

"Oh, funny!" Berne sneered.

"Bernard, do you think you could stop," Lloyd Kingston appealed to his son, before directing a sharp glance at Daniel. "Daniel, I said you could go."

Daniel didn't move, but there was a coolness in his eyes. "No offence, Mr. Kingston, but I work for *Ms* Kingston."

"I prefer Daniel to stay for the moment, Uncle Lloyd," Sandra broke in. "I mightn't have been here today only for him."

"Quite so, quite so." Lloyd Kingston gained control of himself quickly. "But this *is* family business, after all. Please, come and sit down. Elsa, you'll join us?"

"Thank you," Elsa said in a stilted voice.

Berne followed suit. "So what are your plans?" he fired off at Sandra. "You're going to sell the place?"

"What does it matter to you, Bernie?" Sandra asked, sinking into a deep leather armchair.

"It matters a lot. You seem to have forgotten Grandad gave Dad and me the right to remain here for as long as we want."

"Elsa, too," Sandra reminded him, turning her head to smile at the other woman. "I didn't think you'd want to stay, Bernie. Unless you've changed a good deal you hate station life?"

Berne's face so much like his father's darkened. "Don't tell us you intend to keep the place going? As if you could!" he added scornfully.

"Maybe *I* couldn't on my own, but Daniel can until such time I put a professional manager in place. That's if Daniel doesn't want to stay."

Berne gazed from one to the other. "You're pretty cosy aren't you? Daniel this, Daniel that."

"Oh, do get a grip on yourself, Bernard," his father implored. "You can't waste your life like I have. Sandra is right. You're no more suited to station work than I am. Dad knew that."

"That is no reason why he should have left Moondai to Sandra," Berne responded hotly, his thin cheeks flushed. "What the hell does *she* know? Less than either of us. It's all so unfair. We can't even contest it. Dad's lawyer told us it'd be a waste of time."

"Have you ever known your grandfather to get legal matters wrong?" Lloyd asked very dryly. It appeared, unlike his son, he was in a conciliatory mood. "Dad spent a lot of time in Brisbane in the months before he died. He meant then to cut us out.

Trevor's daughter was to get Moondai. Trevor, after all, was his favourite son. *I* never did measure up."

"I didn't think *I* did, either," Sandra said. "Grandad's will was as big a shock to me as it was to you."

"I bet it wasn't a shock to Daniel here," Berne's handsome face was twitching with pent-up anger.

"Meaning?" Daniel's powerful, lean body stirred restlessly.

"You know exactly what I mean," Berne exploded. "You, after all, were in my grandfather's confidence. He had such faith in you. You were damn near the grandson he never had. Was he hatching some plan, do you suppose? The cogs and wheels never stopped turning. Sandra was his heiress. *You* were the sort of guy who could take over the reins. You've proved to be very successful running Moondai and while you were at it, running rings around me, deliberately showing me up. Dad's an old dinosaur. All he wants to do is study his stupid plants."

"So what *are* you saying, Berne?" Lloyd Kingston broke in testily.

"I'm not a fool, Dad," he exploded, showing no respect for his father at all. "I've gone over and over this. Either Grandad expected that without him the whole place would go to wrack and ruin or he could fit Sandra up with a suitable husband. A lot of people in the know seem to think Daniel here is outstanding. He's a real go-getter. He never stops working to impress. Yet he's a nothing and a no-one. Dirt poor until Grandad gave him a leg up. For all we know, Grandad could have extracted a promise from Dan to look out for Sandra. *Marry* her. Take on the Kingston name. It's been done before today. He certainly felt no woman could run Moondai. Sandra's not even a woman. Just look at her! She's hardly grown since she was ten."

"I have, Bernie," Sandra assured him. "I don't apologise for being petite. You know what they say. Good things come in small packages. I'm all grown-up, *unlike* you. Just so you know I graduated with honours from university with a B.A. majoring in psychology among other things. Consequently I find this theory of yours of considerable interest. Daniel is signed up to be my hero. Is that it?"

"Doesn't look like you're too uncomfortable with it," Berne snorted.

"Well *I* am," Daniel said, his eyes luminous with anger. "You're talking drivel, Berne, but then you seldom talk anything else. I fully expected Mr. Kingston to leave Moondai to your father who could have hired top management to run the station had he wanted. My windfall turned out to be at least as big a surprise. Mr. Kingston never once mentioned his granddaughter to me."

"You expect us to believe that?" Berne was the picture of outraged disbelief. "You always had your heads together. Every time I saw you, you were going into a huddle."

"You don't run a station this size sitting on your backside, Berne." Daniel didn't bother to hide his disgust. "Your grandfather always had areas of concern for me to address. They were *all* about station management and business. Which reminds me instead of standing here listening to wild scenarios I should see what's been happening in my absence. The men like to have their duties for the day laid out."

Sandra tried for eye-to-eye contact, failed. "But you haven't had anything to eat, Daniel," she reminded him, loath to see him go.

"Don't worry about me." He gave her a brief salute and turned on his heel.

Sandra made no apologies to the others. She went after him, catching him in the hallway. "I'm sorry about all that, Daniel," she panted. "Bernie has always been a jealous, resentful creature."

"And he talks a lot of drivel. I'd advise you not to listen."

"You're angry?" Carefully she approached him, touching his arm. It was rigid with tension.

"You bet I am!" He stared down into her face. "This isn't going to work, Sandra. I want to help you out, but I'm not going to cop the likes of Berne. Your uncle's arrogance only adds fuel to the flames."

"Why put them before me?" she retorted. "I

need help, Daniel. I need it from *you*. Please tell me I have it?"

"Hell!" Daniel was grappling with her potent effect on him. All this woman magic shouldn't be allowed.

"You're more than a match for both of them put together," she cajoled him, giving him a soulful look.

"No need to pour it on." He stared back challengingly into those blue, *blue,* eyes, his own expression somewhat grim. "The *real* question is, Ms Kingston. Am I a match for *you!*"

CHAPTER FIVE

IT WAS a dismal lunch though the food was good. Meg, looking almost exactly the same, but a little plumper, had come to the library door all smiles. Sandra had no hesitation going into her arms.

"Sandy!" Tears brimmed in the housekeeper's eyes. "It's wonderful to have you back."

It wasn't possible to say, "Wonderful to be back," instead Sandra settled for, "It's wonderful to see you, Meg. I've never forgotten you or your kindnesses to me and my mother."

"I wrote to you, dear."

Sandra shook her head, frowning slightly. "I didn't get any letters."

"I didn't think you did." Meg sounded unsurprised. "Anyway, you're back and I'm thrilled."

"Do we have to listen to any more gushing?" Berne burst out. "I'm hungry."

"You must try to do something about yourself, Bernard," his father said, regarding his son with disappointed eyes. "You'll never get what you want out of life if you continue to be so belligerent."

"And *you* have, Dad, I suppose?" Berne scowled.

Sandra waited for another reprimand, but none came.

Meg had set up lunch in the breakfast room which had a high beamed ceiling and a lovely view of the rear garden with its stands of lemon scented gums. Roast chicken was on the menu, cold cuts, potato salad and a green salad enlivened by a Thai chilli dressing. Sandra had deliberately not chosen the carver at the head of the mahogany table which could seat ten. She guessed correctly her uncle had laid claim to that. She sat to his right with Berne opposite her and Elsa way off at the other end of the table though Sandra had tried to coax her to sit closer. It was clear Elsa had made an art form out of staying near invisible when she could easily have kicked over the traces and spent the rest of her time travelling the world, first class.

It soon transpired Uncle Lloyd was set on his course of reconciliation—or the appearances thereof—but after a limited amount of time spent on pleasantries—including kind enquiries about Pamela, once so dreadfully maligned—Berne began to worry away at Sandra's inheritance and her future plans like a dog with a bone.

"Obviously you've got some idea what you intend

to do with Moondai?" Fiercely he stabbed at a small chunk of new potato.

"Give me a break, Bernie," Sandra said. "I've only just arrived."

"Wonder of wonders!" He rolled his eyes.

"You can say that again! Only Daniel's such a good pilot or I could be dead or in hospital in a coma. As I've already said, I had no idea Grandad would make me the major beneficiary in his will. After all, he sent Mum and me packing, remember?"

"He should never have done that." Elsa startled them by offering the stern comment.

"No, he shouldn't!" Sandra showed her own deeply entrenched resentments.

"Come off it, Sandra." Berne's smile was acid. "Your mother was a real tart! No offence."

His father broke in. "This has gone far enough, Bernard. I insist you keep a civil tongue in your head. Apologise to Sandra right now."

"Dad, you must be joking!" Berne sat back astounded. "Aren't *you* the one who called Aunty Pam every dirty name you could think of? So now you're going to make nice?"

Colour stained Lloyd Kingston's strongly defined cheekbones. "That was in the past, Bernard. I was only teasing anyway."

"Teasing?" Berne shouted with laughter that held no trace of humour.

Sandra for her part felt a swift surge of anger. "My

mother suffered from your taunts, Uncle Lloyd. So did I. Now, if *I* am willing to let bygones be bygones I hope you'll do the same. I didn't make myself Grandad's heiress. Grandad did. I have no idea what was going through his mind—"

"Boy, that's rich!" Berne lounged back. "I gave you a reason. Every time I came on Grandad and Daniel they were locked into deep conversation. He'd turned his back on Dad and me. We didn't measure up. He *knew* Dad would sell Moondai like a shot if he got his hands on it. I would, too."

"What about Elsa?" Sandra asked, looking in Elsa's direction. "Elsa is Grandad's widow."

Berne looked stunned. "Elsa could never take over. She can't even handle the dinner menu as I'm sure she'll agree. Meg runs the house."

"Why are you speaking like this, Bernie?" Sandra asked. It was so unkind and disrespectful.

"It doesn't matter, Alexandra!" Elsa said, waving a thin hand.

"But Elsa it *does* matter," Sandra said. "Anyway Meg *is* the housekeeper. Before you married my grandfather you were a successful businesswoman. Didn't you miss it?"

Elsa seemed to shrink in her carver chair. "That was a lifetime ago, Alexandra."

"Does one truly lose one's skills or the need to use them?"

"My cleverness has diminished with the years,"

Elsa said. "I know you mean to be kind, Alexandra, but nothing Bernard says affects me."

"Is that so?" Berne intervened with heavy sarcasm. "If the truth were known, Elsa, you *lost* it the day you married Grandad. Grandad didn't want a career woman with a mind and a life of her own. He wanted a woman who would know her place, not a business partner. That's when you set about turning yourself into a piece of furniture."

"Really, are you any better?" Elsa asked, piercing him with her colourless eyes. "You strut around doing next to nothing while Daniel runs everything. Gutless young men like you disgust me."

Berne's face was a study. "Well what do you know?" he chortled. "She *can* talk."

"Rudeness is what you employ, Bernard, instead of brains," Elsa said gravely. "I have never wished to talk to you."

"Ditto!" Berne retaliated, dark eyes flashing. "I'm lighting out of here as soon as I'm ready. Who am I anyway? *No one!*"

Sandra, amazed by the exchange between Elsa and Berne, felt a sudden rush of empathy for her cousin. "Look, I'm sorry, Bernie," she said. "I'm sorry Grandad cut you out. I'm sorry he did the same to Uncle Lloyd. He was a very strange man."

"He was that!" Elsa pulled more wisps out of her bundle of hair. "He should have been had up for mental cruelty."

"Struth!" Berne dug his fork into a piece of chicken like he wanted to spear someone. "Don't be so ungrateful, Elsa. Grandad's life may not have centred around *you,* but he made sure you were kept very comfortable in your quiet corner. He did leave you rich if not merry."

"Which was only fitting," Sandra murmured.

"If I could I'd send it back to him in hell," Elsa told them bleakly. "It wasn't *money* I wanted from Rigby. It wasn't *money* the rest of you wanted from him, either. It was love and attention. There were only two people Rigby loved in this world. Catherine and Trevor. The rest of us amounted to a big fat nothing."

"Well thank you for sharing that with us, Elsa," Lloyd said suavely. "I must say I too have been missing the sound of your voice. Perhaps Sandra's arrival has brought it back?"

"Why not?" Elsa nodded her head. "I was fond of her father. He was very different to you, Lloyd." Her colourless gaze shifted to Sandra. "It's a great burden you've taken on, Alexandra. This place killed your father."

"Oh for pity's sake!" Lloyd Kingston fetched up a great sigh. "Please don't start on that, Elsa. I won't have it."

"My mother believes to this day my father's death wasn't an accident," Sandra found herself saying although she hadn't intended to.

"And what do you believe, Sandra?" her uncle asked while Elsa turned her head away, looking extremely distressed.

"Can you truly say you weren't my father's enemy?" Sandra looked directly into her uncle's hooded dark eyes.

Lloyd Kingston's face flushed a dark red. "I'm going to forgive you for that, Sandra. That's your mother talking. You were a child. Your mother filled your head with terrible stories. It was a way of getting back at me for the things I'd said about her. A lot of which was true by the way. I loved your father, my brother. I looked up to him. He was everything I wasn't just as Elsa so kindly said. And he had a *heart* which Dad never had. I never regarded Trevor as the enemy. That's blasphemy. I don't regard *anyone* as my enemy."

"Not *me,* Uncle Lloyd?" Sandra asked, quietly.

"Especially not you," he answered without hesitation. "You're Trevor's child."

"Sure about that, Dad?" Berne asked in a taunting voice. "If I were Sandra I'd be worried about what lay behind your sleek mask. No one in this family ever tells the truth."

"How very true," Elsa said in a heartfelt voice, brushing long fingers through her hair. "It is only justice you inherited Moondai, Alexandra. It would have gone to your father."

Sandra bit hard on her lip. After a moment, she rose

from the table, saying quietly, "Please excuse me. I'd like to look around this afternoon. I'll take the Jeep out the front if that's okay?" She pushed in her chair, holding the back of it while she got out what she had to say. "I've asked Daniel to move out of the overseer's bungalow and into the house for a while."

As she expected, there was a stunned silence. She might just as well have said the authorities had handed over to her the most dangerous felon in the country to be housed.

Berne finally broke the silence. "You've *what?*"

"Sandra, is that *wise?*" Lloyd asked with less intensity, but he too looked shocked.

Sandra shrugged. "Elsa has no objection. Daniel can have my old bedroom. It's only until I bring myself up to scratch on station affairs. He'll be a big help there as Grandad intended. I'll move into my parents' old suite."

"I'm quite happy to move out of the master suite," Lloyd Kingston offered. "You have only to say the word."

"Sandra isn't going to say it, Dad, just as you were counting on. What you *weren't* counting on was that Sandra is no fool. She wasn't easily fooled as a kid, either."

Sandra was surprised by his support, if indeed that's what it was. She decided to hold out an olive branch. "I don't suppose you'd like to drive around with me, Bernie?"

For the first time he looked uncertain of himself. "You can't want me surely?"

"What's the sense in us not being friends? We're cousins. We can adapt."

Berne considered that one, in the end succumbing to his overload of resentments. "Not overnight we can't!" He shook his head sharply. "Thanks for the offer. It's beyond me right now to accept."

In the kitchen she spoke to Meg about room arrangements asking Meg to make up some sandwiches for Daniel's lunch. Meg too looked surprised when told Daniel would be staying at the house for a time, but in no way did she appear dismayed. Rather she appeared firmly onside.

"What is it, love? Are you nervous?" she asked shrewdly, long used to the warring Kingstons.

Sandra gave a wry laugh. "I have powerfully bad memories of this place, Meg. Daniel is a big dependable guy. I'd like him around. Besides, it's quite true I'll be relying heavily on him to teach me what I need to know about the station."

"Well he can do that," Meg said, slicing off some ham. "Towards the end he was your grandfather's right hand man. You could say your grandad treated him as more a grandson than he did Berne."

"That must have been awful for Berne?" Despite everything she felt twinges of pity for her cousin.

"It wasn't good." Meg shook her head. "It's time

for Bernie to make a life of his own. He's got no direction. It's my belief, excuse me, Sandy for saying this, but inherited wealth is death to ambition. Most times anyway."

It was amazing how quickly it was all coming back to her. Sitting tall behind the wheel of the Jeep Sandra drove out of the home compound taking the broad gravelled drive that wound past the neat and comfortable staff bungalows and bunkhouses. Station employees materialized out of nowhere, roughly lining the track. She began to wave. They all waved back. There were mothers with little children, groundsmen, stockmen, what looked like station mechanics going on their oil stained overalls. Finally she stopped the Jeep and climbed out.

"Hi! Lovely to see you all. I'm Sandra, back home again."

Her youth, the diminutive size of her, the smile on her face and the friendliness of her tone instantly broke the ice. People surged at her, delighted and determined to meet the new boss personally. They had all known she was coming. Mr. Kingston's will— what they knew of it—had been discussed at great length and gasped over. What was going to happen to Moondai, to their jobs? They all knew about the forced landing of the station helicopter in the swamp. Daniel had spoken to his foreman as well as Lloyd Kingston up at the house. The foreman relayed the news to the crew. In a small closely knit settlement like Moondai news travelled faster than an emu at full gallop.

Rigby Kingston had been one thing. His grand-daughter was proving to be very much another. Instead of leaping briskly out of the way or averting their eyes if their former Boss was about in one of his dark moods, his granddaughter was happy being surrounded by smiling faces. Some faces Sandra re-membered and greeted by name. Others, the young wives and the small children were newcomers to Moondai. Sandra found herself nursing babies, which she loved, accepting invitations to morning tea and paying a visit to the schoolhouse where all the children on the station under ten were offered an education by a well qualified teacher. With these open-faced smiling people around her Sandra felt safe.

By the time she drove on she was feeling quite cheerful, not realising friendliness and a genuine interest in the people around them was a side of the Kingston character that had seldom emerged since her father's day.

I could almost build a life here, she thought. That was the voice of her heart. But what of her head? These people liked her at any rate. Drat her family.

One of the station hands had told her Daniel's location. He was out at the crater, a natural amphi-theatre caused by massive earth movements hundred of millions of years before. The family had always used that name for the grassy basin which was almost enclosed—save for a broad canyon—by low lying rugged cliffs of reddish quartzite and sandstone. It was quite possible to climb to the highest point which their Kingston forefather had named Mount Alexandra after his wife. The same Alexandra Sandra had been named for. Of course it wasn't a mountain at all. More a hill, but it *reared* out of the vast perfectly flat plains so its height was accentuated. The climb to the summit was a stiff hike too and dangerous with all the falling rubble, but the view from the top Sandra could still remember.

Her father had used to sing to her that they were sitting on top of the world, his arm around her sheltering her from the strong winds.

Why did you go and die on me, Dad? Why? Why did you leave me? It was hard. So hard. Do you know the things that have happened to me? How frightened I was without you to protect me? How much I hated Jem?

She often found herself talking to her father. Not out loud of course, but in her mind. Sometimes she thought he answered. She talked to her little friend, Nikki, too, asking her what it was like in the kingdom of Heaven. Was it all it was cracked up to be? If anyone deserved eternal joy it was Nikki and the children like Nikki who had been so brave and cheerful it had put her own troubles into perspective.

Her father hadn't wanted to die, either. She couldn't forgive her uncle, for all she had said about letting bygones be bygones. Life didn't work that way. The past could never be buried so deeply it couldn't resurrect itself at a moment's notice. All it needed was the requisite trigger.

The light was dazzling. She pushed her akubra further down over her eyes, congratulating herself she'd had the foresight to buy one from a Western outfitter in Brisbane. It had been hard getting one her size especially when she no longer had her mop of curls to help prop it up. Best quality lens sunglasses sat on her nose, though in the heat they were continually sliding down the bridge. She remembered this extraordinary dazzle of light, blinding in its brilliance, the cloudless skies, the golden spinifex and the blood red sands the wind could sweep into the most beautiful and fascinating delicate whorls and patterns. She remembered the way the desert bloomed in profusion after the rains; the great vistas of the white and yellow paperdaisies she particularly loved; the magnificent sight of the burning sun going down on the Macdonnell Ranges that were always overhung by a hue of grape-blue. These ranges of the Wild Heart were once sand on the beach of the inland sea the early explorers had searched for in vain. She loved the way the wild donkeys came out to graze at sunset and whole colonies of rabbits popped out of their warrens keeping a sharp lookout for any dingoes on the prowl. Around Moondai all the dingoes had been purebred. A wild dingo in prime condition was a splendid sight, but one always had to remember they were killers by nature.

A big mob of cattle was being walked not far from a waterhole where legions of budgies and perky little zebra finches were having a drink, indifferent to the presence of a falcon that coasted overhead making itself ready for a leisurely swoop. Kill and be killed, she thought. There were always predators, always victims. Her mind returned to the question of what had caused the mechanical components in the tail section of the helicopter to work their way loose. Daniel had explained it but it hadn't been all that easy for a nonmechanically minded person like herself to take in. Had someone deliberately inter-fered with the control system, or had it simply been another case of mechanical failure? So many people over the years had been killed in the Outback when helicopters or light aircraft crashed either soon after take-off, or attempting to land. Some plowed into rugged ranges while others took a nosedive to the desert floor. Flying was a risky business especially over the heated unpredictable air of the desert, but given the vast distances flying was no luxury; it was a way of life.

It was the greatest good fortune that Daniel was such a good helicopter pilot. He had to be equally good with fixed-wing although she understood flying a helicopter was quite different to flying a fixed-wing aircraft. Daniel was licensed to fly both as was Berne. She wasn't sure if her uncle flew the helicopter, but he had always held a pilot's licence as had her father and grandfather. It occurred to her it might be a good idea for her to start taking lessons. She had to overcome her fears if she really intended to stay on Moondai. Maybe in the process she would unveil a new aspect of herself?

The drive through the broad canyon was an experience in itself. The walls presented an extravaganza of brilliant dry ochres, fiery reds, russets, pinks, yellows, stark glaring white with carved shadows of amethyst. High up in every available pocket of earth the hardy spinifex had taken root. Because of the recent rains many clumps were a fresh green, most a dull gold. The sandy floor of the canyon was as red as boiling magma, giving vital clues to the mighty explosion that had formed the crater aeons ago. To either side of the canyon long tranquil chains of waterholes already beginning to dry out sparkled in the sun. In the gums nearby, preening or dozing amid the abundant fresh olive foliage were great numbers of the pink and grey galahs who made sure they were always in the vicinity of water. She had grown up with all this even if she had lost contact over the years. Only love of this ancient land was in her bloodstream hence her deeply felt response. Time and distance had not altered the old magic.

The crater, secret to all save the aborigines for tens of thousands of years was a miracle of nature. It attracted massive flocks of birds and wildlife. It was wonderful to look out over the giant bowl of the crater with its protected grasslands then up at the rounded curves, peaks and swells of the surrounding rim.

That afternoon the natural amphitheatre was thickly carpeted in grasses that were liberally strewn with the wildflowers and spider lilies that thrived in the semi-desert environment. Her favourites, the everlastings which didn't wilt when picked, were by far in the majority. In one area she drove through to get to the holding yards they were pink, then a mile or so on, bright yellow interspersed with long trailing branches of crimson desert peas, native poppies, hibiscus, fire bush, hop bush, salt bush, emu bush. There were so many she couldn't begin to name them. She had to leave that to Uncle Lloyd who loved every living thing that grew in the earth far more than people. Cataloguing all this floral splendour was his passion. The ranges at their back door harboured a great wealth of wildflowers, making them an exciting hunting ground for a man who was both amateur botanist and excellent photographer. She remembered her father saying with admiration how his brother, Lloyd, had an encyclopaedic knowledge of the flora of the Red Centre and

Queensland's Channel Country where he had spent a lot of time. Did a botanist, passionate about wild-flowers, morph into a murderer? It didn't seem possible.

She brought the Jeep to a halt a little distance from the pens. To one side she could see a calf cradle, a ratchet locking device that restrained the calves due for earmarking, branding, dehorning and castration. She slid out of the Jeep and stood with her back against the passenger door watching Daniel stride towards her. Back in the city any guy that looked like him would be mobbed on a daily basis she thought with wry amusement. She had never seen anyone so young exude so much authority. It was strange to think Daniel didn't know who his father was. He had to be a six footer plus, strikingly handsome. From which parent had come those extraordinary eyes? They were the colour of sun on water.

"Hi!" He sketched a salute, forefinger to the brim of his cream akubra.

"Hi, Daniel," she replied, not a whit disconcerted by the way he towered over her. Authority emanated from Daniel, never menace. "When you stalked off, you missed lunch so I brought you some sandwiches."

"Now aren't you kind." He smiled at her, wondering if her beautiful skin was as cool and soft as it looked. "The men are about due for a break. I'll get Nat to make us a cup of tea. You can meet the men in the break."

"I'd like that," she said, following him over to an area of deep shade. The thick stubby grass that surrounded the tall gums was studded with the all embracing wildflowers, their pretty faces brighter in the refreshing shade. The men had looked up at her arrival, but when she looked back, they had their heads down, hard at work.

Nat turned out to be a wiry jackeroo of around twenty whose duties included making the billy tea for the men when they were out on the job. He had recently perfected an old-fashioned camp fire damper which he offered to Sandra spread with lashings of jam. She accepted tea and the damper with a smile not about to tell him she rarely drank tea and never ate jam. Somehow she'd choke it down.

She and Daniel made themselves comfortable beneath the shadiest tree, Sandra thinking there was no one she'd rather share the moment with. How did one reach such a point so early in a friendship? she thought in some wonderment. All she was absolutely certain of, was, she *had*.

Daniel, oblivious to her soul searching, opened out his packet of sandwiches kept fresh by cling wrap. "These look good," he said appreciatively, getting a kick out of the fact she had thought of him. But then she was thoughtful. And very kind. He remembered her little friend Nikki and the sacrifice Sandra had made of her crowning glory.

"Eat up!" she said happily.

His smile was beautiful. The towering gums were beautiful, the crush of wildflowers at their feet were beautiful. The cooling breeze was beautiful, the aromatic smell of the camp fire. *Everything* was beautiful she thought ecstatically.

"You must be hungry?" She stretched out a little, revelling in the vast landscape.

He held a protective hand over the package. "I'll just down a few of these before you start to pinch them."

"It's okay. I had lunch."

"How did it go?" He shot her a sidelong glance thinking her profile was like a perfect cameo.

Sandra swallowed a mouthful of tea, finding it surprisingly good. "Uncle Lloyd was in a conciliatory mood. Bernie was Bernie and Elsa made a few surprising comments that struck home. As a child I couldn't make her out. I can't now. She's so *quiet*, but I have the feeling a lot is going on in her head."

"Well it can't be *good*. She looks positively haunted to me." Daniel picked up another sandwich, deriving a great deal of pleasure in the company of his new boss. Even in the heat of the afternoon she was as bright and fresh as the daisies that ringed them round. She had a tiny beauty spot high up on her right cheekbone just beneath the outer corner of her eye. It emphasized the porcelain perfection of her skin and the natural darkness of her lashes and brows. Quite a contrast with the buttercup coloured hair that clung to her beautifully shaped skull. Not many could look so good with so little hair.

Sandra, while endeavouring to appear not to, was intensely aware of his leisurely inspection and was just as intensely satisfied. She *wanted* him to notice her. She was actively *willing* it. "Why are you looking at me like that?" she asked.

He laughed. "May a cat not look at the queen?"

"I suppose so if it gets the opportunity. This damper is very good but I don't actually eat jam. Would you like it? Then I can have one of those sandwiches."

"Which one?" he asked with an amused look on his face.

"Oh any! I couldn't get my tongue around lunch although I was hungry. Bernie was shouting and shoving his chair around. It put me off."

"I don't want the damper, either," he told her, passing a ham and mustard sandwich and looking Nat's way. "I'll eat just about anything when I'm hungry but *not* damper. It sticks in my chest."

"You'll have to eat it," she said. "We don't want to offend him."

He shook his head carelessly. "He'll get over it. So did you tell them you want me to move into the house?"

She tossed her head back. "I said you'd fit in like you belonged there."

"Like hell I will!" he muttered beneath his breath.

"No matter, you're doing *me* a great service. Elsa took the news with great equanimity. She can't have much fun with Uncle Lloyd and Bernie who, predictably, had serious misgivings."

He drained his mug of tea. "Please don't tell me on a beautiful day like this."

"It *is* a beautiful day, isn't it?" She gave a voluptuous sigh, looking utterly relaxed. A gorgeous butterfly drifted by just to add to her happiness. "You can smell all the wildflowers!" She inhaled. "I used to love Moondai when I was a kid."

"Why wouldn't you? It's a part of you." He was entranced and entertained by her ever changing expressions. She might be small but there was a lot of life in her.

"I know that now. Daniel, why do you suppose my mother thought Uncle Lloyd wanted to get rid of my dad? Uncle Lloyd is a passionate botanist for God's sake."

"I can't imagine him killing anyone, Sandra." While Daniel didn't have a lot of time for Sandra's uncle, he had to say what he believed.

"He wouldn't have to do it himself," she pointed out.

"No." He was deeply sceptical. "Your uncle isn't the most likable man in the world. He's an appalling snob, but not, I think, a murderer."

"Who then?" she asked. "Bernie has more hangups than I have, but he was just a kid. Elsa? I can't imagine Elsa turning into a homicidal maniac. Marrying Grandad had to be one of the worst decisions she ever made. She mustn't have wanted a man who would play around like her first husband. Sex creates tremendous problems."

Daniel leaned back, the more to study her. "When it's good it beats most things," he offered casually.

"I beg your pardon?" Her heart started to make wild little flutters in her chest.

"You don't agree?" One eyebrow shot up sardonically.

She coloured up. "You keep waiting for me to make a slip."

"I do." He looked at her with a mixture of gentle mockery and indulgence.

"Well you're not ever going to hear it," she promised.

"And here I am the soul of discretion," he said. "Your secrets are safe with me, Alexandra. Anyway we were talking about more momentous things. Who hated your dad enough to want to see him dead? We already know yours is a highly dysfunctional family but I think you'd have to rule them out. It was an accident, pure and simple. Now you're a woman as opposed to the child, you have to accept that. Your mother would have been in a highly emotional state. She probably hated your uncle as much as he hated her."

"He was right about her behaviour when she was

away from us," Sandra stared down at the tea leaves at the bottom of her tin mug as though the random arrangement held answers. "Mother was a bad, bad, girl. She's highly susceptible to male admiration to this day. I didn't see it then of course. I heard what Uncle Lloyd was saying but I couldn't understand what he was getting at. Heck, I was only a kid. What I *did* take in was the way he questioned whether Dad was my father or not."

"Now that's really wicked." Daniel gave his judgment. "And just plain wrong."

"Sometimes I wanted to attack him with a meat axe," Sandra confided, watching the beautiful butterfly, a marvellous blue, make another circuit of their heads.

Daniel ran his thumb along his lean jaw. "You're a blood-thirsty little thing. I just hope I never fall out with you."

She jabbed him in the arm. "You must never, *never,* do that, Daniel."

"Even if it's a lot to ask?"

He didn't smile. He appeared to be taking her seriously. "Even then." She nodded as though she could see into the future. "You've signed on for another year. I won't be twenty-one until August. A journey of six months. You have to stick around for another six after that."

"Will do. Hey, sit still," he urged in a hushed tone. "What is it? What's the matter?"

He sat up straight. "A butterfly has been hovering around. It's alighted on your head. Probably thinks it's a chrysanthemum."

"Oooh!" She drew in her breath and held it. "Is it still there?"

"Want me to catch it?"

"You might damage its wings."

"No, I won't!"

He sounded very sure. Still she shut her eyes. When she opened them again, their heads were very close together, the sable and the golden yellow. "All right, ready?" he murmured.

"Ready."

He opened his hand slowly, revealing the butterfly in all its beauty. It clung to the skin of his hand for barely a second, brilliant blue, yellow and black wings with a glinting yellow body, before it flew off.

"Surely that's a good omen," she whispered, staring into his eyes. They were so close she held her breath. This man was *beautiful!* He made her insides ache.

"I'm sure it is," Daniel said just as softly.

Something in his eyes, in his voice, made a thousand tingles run up and down her spine. Neither of them moved—it was as though movement was impossible—then Daniel pulled back, casualness falling over his intense expression.

Sandra followed his lead, though the tingles hadn't gone away. She sat back, her shoulders pressed against the trunk of the tree. "By the way,

Grandad didn't approach you with any deal, did he?" she asked after a moment.

"What sort of deal, Ms Kingston?" He was all crisp attention.

"Oh forget it," she said, taking swift note of the crease between his brows. "Just me being paranoid. Bernie took one hell of a crack on the head when he was a kid. Fell off his horse. Maybe that explains why he too is wandering around in an emotional fog." She broke off, as the stockmen started coming around for their afternoon tea break. "Time to meet the men," she said.

"Right you are, ma'am." Daniel stood up, offering her his hand. "Some of them were around when you left."

"I've already met quite a few people on my way out here," she told him. Now the tingles spread from her spine to her hand, to *everywhere!* "I loved the babies. I've been invited to a getting to know you morning tea. The schoolteacher wants me to look in on the lessons. I mean to meet everyone on the station. That includes the aboriginal people who pass through on walkabout."

"Seems more and more like you intend to stay?"

"Who knows!" She took a very deep breath. "One thing I do know with certainty. My life has changed forever."

CHAPTER SIX

DANIEL had been expecting a bedroom modest in size—or as modest as the rooms at Moondai homestead could get—and furnished in a way that reflected the taste of a very young girl. Maybe not lots of pink, painted furniture, decorations, a collection of dolls and so forth, given Sandra's self confessed tomboy qualities. What he got was the stuff of dreams. Ms Alexandra Kingston's childhood bedroom was very large and very grand. So large in fact she must have been lost in it.

"Think you can get used to it?" She circled the huge four poster bed with its draped canopy, giving the beautiful embroidered silk cover several good thumps while she was at it. "Dressing room adjoining, the bathroom pretty small for a big man but it will do."

"I'm sure." He looked about him with the same sense of wonder he had once felt wandering around an Adelaide art gallery. The bedroom walls were hung with paintings. Not any old paintings. He had a naturally good eye, or so he had been told, but art works as good as the ones he was looking at immediately declared their quality. A magnificent antique chest stood at the foot of the bed. She could easily have hidden in it as a child. Maybe even now. A splendid crystal chandelier hung above his head.

"Baccarat," Sandra said nonchalantly, as he tilted his head.

"Of course, Baccarat!" he mocked. He'd never seen anything like it before.

There was a big comfortable cushion laden sofa upholstered in the same gold silk as the bedspread, two armchairs to match and a wing back chair covered in a bold tapestry obviously designed for a man. "I had the wing back chair brought in especially for you," she explained, moving to grace it.

"Not many people have a bedroom like this," he said, brushing long darkly tanned fingers across the pile of a cushion.

"I didn't want my bedroom to look like anybody else's," she said.

His mouth twisted. "You certainly got your wish. What is extraordinary is, you wanted all this when you were what—?"

Sandra rested her bright yellow head against the striking tapestry, the fabric a complementary mix of golds, bronzes and deep crimsons. "Around eight, I guess. I asked my dad if I could have a look around the stuff in the storeroom and he said, 'I'll come with you.' We picked the furniture together. I spotted the chandelier in a big box. Dad had it repaired and in no time at all it was up."

"Where was your mother when all this was happening?" he asked thinking her father's sudden death must have left a tremendous void in her life.

"Oh around," she said vaguely. "Mama said my taste was unbelievable."

"It was very exotic for a small girl."

"That's exactly what I wanted. Exotic, like the old travel books I read in the library. Something from an Arabian bazaar or Aladdin's Cave. Don't you just love the Persian rug under your feet?"

"Don't tell me." He moved backwards so he could study the central medallion and the floral arabesques. "It flies?"

"No, no," she said, laughing. "It's a late nineteenth-century Isfahan. My great-great-great-grandmother, Alexandra, was a rich Scottish lassie who was the big collector in the family. That's her portrait over there." She pointed to a large painting of an aristocratic looking young woman with a thick mane of bright red hair, narrow green eyes, very white skin and a pointed chin. She wasn't a beauty, her features were too sharp, but she was certainly striking as was her richly decorated dark green velvet dress.

"Nice to have ancestors," he said dryly.

"Have you never tried to find out who your father was, Daniel?" she asked, hearing the darkness in his tone. "I thought you could find out anything these days."

"Did you now?" he said, turning away from this young woman who was right out of his league. Outback royalty no less. Even the ancestor looked impossibly classy. He moved closer to inspect a gilt framed equine painting of a magnificent white Arabian stallion in a half rearing—neck bent stylised pose. In the background beneath a darkening turquoise sky was its dark skinned handler, with a bright red fez on his head. A fine horseman and a great lover of the most beautiful of all animals this was the one painting he coveted.

"French," Sandra said seeing his interest. "Late 1800s. I absolutely love it. Do I take it you tried but got nowhere?"

"Nowhere at all," he said briefly, turning back to face her. Her eyes were like precious gems, so dark a blue in some lights and depending on what she wore, they were violet. Did she know she looked like a painting herself framed by the antique armchair that all but swallowed her up?

"I'm sorry, Daniel," she said, those huge eyes sad and serious.

"I've dealt with it," he said brusquely, wanting yet not wanting her sympathy.

"How?"

"You ask too many questions." He began to prowl around restlessly.

"What happened to your mother?"

He picked up a silver object, put it down again. "She just died. I don't like to talk about it."

"Maybe you should. I hoped you would talk to me. After all I know a lot about death. Your mother must have been very young?"

"She was," he said sombrely, wanting her to leave it alone. "But I can hold on to her memory."

"Yes, you can," she agreed, turning her face more fully towards him. "I remember as clearly as though it were yesterday the afternoon my father was buried. All the Kingstons are buried on Moondai."

"I know." He was familiar with the family cemetery where Rigby Kingston had been buried alongside his first wife, Catherine, who had died of cancer, his favourite son, Trevor, not far away; his ancestors around him. His mother's ashes he had tossed on a desert whirlwind for that was what she had wanted. No trace left.

"Of course, you were *there*," Sandra realized. "My grandfather obviously didn't want me at his funeral. Maybe he was trying to spare me something Lord knows! But I held his hand the day my father was buried."

"Did you?" Daniel took a seat on the huge carved chest to listen to her tale. He had never before he met her considered he might fall under the spell of Ms Alexandra Kingston. She was his employer for one thing. She was too young, unattainable to the likes of him, but everything about her gave him immense pleasure, the more so every time he saw her. "Why not your mother's hand?" he asked, really wanting to know.

"Mama went to pieces," she explained. "She was crying all the time. I remember someone I didn't know was standing beside her holding her up."

"Man or woman?"

"What do you think?" Her response was laconic. "I remember his glossy black shoes. I held Grandad's hand and he let me even though he didn't like holding hands. Everyone was in black but I wore my best dress, the one Dad liked. It was bright yellow. I tied my hair back with a yellow ribbon. When they lowered the coffin I wanted to jump in with him. I know Grandad wanted to jump in, too. He nearly broke my fingers he held them so tight. Mama was crying buckets, but Grandad and I saved our tears for later."

"What about your uncle Lloyd? Can you remember what he was like that day?"

Sandra shut her eyes tight the better to summon up the memory. "He didn't cry, either, but he looked terrible. He threw something in. Some little leather-bound book. I threw in a letter I wrote and the gold cup I'd just won at a riding competition at the Alice. Mum threw in a red rose. It made Grandad very angry but he never showed it until later."

"That must have been a terrible day for you, Sandra."

She pressed a hand to her fragile temple. "Maybe that's one of the reasons I trust you, Daniel. We both know about terrible days. And we both lost a dad."

"You can't miss what you never had." Daniel shrugged, which was a lie. "At least you were blessed with your memories of him." He stood up abruptly, tall and strong, suppressed emotion in his eyes.

I'm starting to get very good at reading Daniel's face, Sandra thought. Underneath the calmness, the quiet authority and the humour was a passionate man. "Want to see my room?" She whipped herself into sudden action.

"Now that's an offer! I can't refuse." He caught the fresh scent of her as she all but danced by him, light and graceful as any ballerina.

"I want to do lots of things to it," she confided. "It's much too staid. I bet you thought you were going to sleep in baby bear's bed?"

He laughed. "I never thought for a minute you'd let me into anywhere so grand."

"I need you to be happy, Daniel," she said seriously, walking through the open doorway of her parents' old suite while Daniel followed, keeping a few paces behind.

The suite was massive, very traditional in design with a colour scheme of bluish-grey and cream. A few paintings hung on the wall—nothing like the eclectic collection in Sandra's room but a beautiful, eye catching Chinoiserie screen stood beside the white marble fireplace. Over the mantle hung an oil and pencil drawing of a lovely little girl around five years of age with huge blue eyes and a cascade of golden ringlets.

"Recognise me?" she asked.

For a moment he said nothing, seized by a violent rush of tenderness that caught him unawares. He wanted to reach out and touch it, study it up close. There was a magical quality about such sweetness and innocence.

"Daniel?" she prompted. He'd had more than enough time to make a comment.

"Let me look at it properly." He stalled for time. "Who painted it?"

"A very clever friend of Dad's who was visiting us. He's a famous architect now. He lives in Singapore."

"It's lovely," he said, after another pause. "And I get to see your curls."

"You can see them better here." She lifted a silver framed photograph off a small circular table which held a collection of other framed photographs and passed it to him.

"This is Nikki?" he asked quietly.

"Yes." Her voice turned husky.

"Thank you for showing it to me." There was a lump in his own throat. He stared down at the recently taken glossy black and white photograph. In it, Sandra's small face was more gently rounded. She was smiling radiantly. A great cloud of blond hair framed her face and tumbled over her shoulders. Her arms were locked around a little girl obviously in the final stages of the childhood leukaemia that had robbed her of life. The child had huge sorrowful dark eyes but a big smile. She was wearing a beanie to cover the cruel effects of chemotherapy.

"How sad can life get?"

Sandra swallowed on a tight throat. "As soon as my affairs are finalised, I'm making a grant to the Leukaemia Foundation for research on paediatric leukaemia."

"You should," he agreed gently. "How did you come to meet Nikki?" He set the framed photograph carefully back on the table.

"It was my last year at uni. A medical school friend rang me one day to ask if I'd consider joining their little group. A few of them entertained sick kids in hospital, played games with them, read to them, sat with them, sang to them, played guitar, anything to take their minds off their suffering. I went along and listened as dying kids poured out their hearts." She broke off a minute to compose herself. "For some reason they wanted to *talk* to me. I think it had something to do with my blond hair and blue eyes. One little kid around four asked Anthony, my friend, who always dressed as a clown if I was an angel. Some of our group cracked up it was all so gut wrenching but I couldn't walk away. The very same day this photo was taken, Anthony shaved off all my hair when he didn't really want to. He was a little bit in love with me. I've got a photo of that as well with all of us laughing and crying at the same time."

"Well now isn't this cosy?" A voice rife with sarcasm shattered the moment of closeness. "I haven't seen so much togetherness in a long, long time."

Daniel threw back his head, his striking face taut but before he could speak Sandra cut in. "I'm not surprised, Bernie," she said, turning towards her cousin. He was smirking and boldly wagging a finger. "Togetherness isn't something I associate with our family. Do you want something?"

Irritation broke over his face. "Call me Berne," he protested. "I was Bernie when I was a kid. I'm Berne now. I prefer it."

"Berne it is," she said crisply. "I was just showing Daniel his room."

"In case neither of you have noticed, this is *yours,*" he said, acidly, somewhat stunned by the obvious rapport between Moondai's overseer and his cousin.

"So it is," she returned sweetly. "After all, Uncle Lloyd has taken over the master suite."

"Why not? He's the rightful master after all," Berne retaliated.

"Grandad didn't seem to think so."

"No, he was too busy scheming with Daniel here, mornings, afternoons, evenings, you name it. Heads together. Black and silver. Grandad always did cut a fine figure. I always thought—"

"Spare us, Berne," Daniel said, his face strangely impassive. "Your thoughts are way off beam. Your grandfather knew he was dying."

"He told you?" Sandra and Berne spoke together,

Daniel nodded in a matter of fact way. "Yes, he did. I was to say nothing to no one and I didn't. It was his wish and his place to tell his family and anyone else he wanted to know. Some days I suppose he thought he mightn't even last until the morrow. But there were orders to be carried out, decisions to be made. He wasn't going to be around to be in charge. Consequently there was a lot to talk about."

"By God you've kept a lot to yourself." Berne hurled the accusation. "My grandfather was good to you. Why?" he demanded, unable to hide his mountain of resentments. "You got paid well enough, so why the quarter of a million?" More than a touch of challenge had entered Berne's voice. "Was that the dowry price? You could have asked a hell of a lot more."

His intention was clearly to goad Daniel into speaking out and perhaps revealing too much but Daniel had assumed a different guise even as Berne spoke; detached, businesslike, official, pretty much like Rigby Kingston had been as boss. "Maybe I'd better leave. I just know you're going to talk absolute drivel."

"Am I now?" The hot blood rose to Berne's high cheekbones, but something in Daniel's body language sent him back to the doorway where he turned for the final word. "Makes sense to me. Think about it, cousin." He shot a glance at Sandra who was balancing some bronze object in her hand as though she meant to throw it. "Make sense to you? Of course you won't get anything out of Daniel on the subject, but denials. But how many girls want to believe their future husbands were bought for them?"

"You don't think the plan a bit tricky, Berne? As far as I'm concerned marriage is the kiss of death. More than half of all marriages today end in divorce. Quite apart from that, how could Grandad possibly imagine he could so easily manipulate two people? Hypothetical question as I don't believe for a minute there's even a grain of truth in your theory."

"There isn't," Daniel confirmed with quiet contempt.

"Don't believe him, cousin," Berne warned, pleased to have stirred up a hornet's nest. "Listen to your inner voice. See it my way and it all starts to make sense. Didn't Grandad love playing God?'

"That he did," Sandra said, wondering if she could

possibly be blinding herself to what she didn't want to see. After all, it did happen. She raked a hand through the silk floss of her hair, wanting to cling to her natural instincts to trust Daniel.

Berne nodded, as though he had won an important point. "You said it. This whole thing smacks of a deal…a marriage of convenience?"

Sandra stared at him while Daniel clenched his fists, looking like he was struggling hard not to lash out. "I'm not bothered by what you think, Berne. Ms Kingston's trust, however, is important to me."

Sandra spoke up. "There's no need to call me Ms Kingston at *any* time, Daniel, I know why you're unwilling to call me by my Christian name in front of the family and staff but it simply doesn't matter to me. I need guidance and I'm willing to take it from you, Daniel. I trust you." For some reason she felt very close to tears, but no way was she going to allow them to fall.

"That's a mistake." Berne frowned fiercely, jealous of her taking sides. "You're a Kingston. *You* own the station. *He's* an employee."

"An indispensable one Berne, lest you forget. I don't have a problem with Daniel calling me Sandra. The *one* person who knew exactly what he intended when he left Moondai to me, was Grandad. Have you bothered to consider he might have wanted to make reparation. After all, he did kick us out."

"With a trust fund," Berne was driven to shouting.

"You weren't chucked out into the snow. Grandad didn't want to lay eyes on you and your playgirl mother but he made sure you were provided for."

All trace of colour left Sandra's cheeks. "You're lying."

"Lying? Why would I be lying?" Berne gave her a weird look. "It's easily proved. Grandad wasn't going to let you starve. You went to all the best schools didn't you? I know you were kicked out of two. You went on to university. Where the hell did you think the money was coming from? Come on tell me. You're supposed to be so bright."

Daniel intervened, holding up his palm to Berne so Sandra could speak. "Did your mother never tell you this, Sandra?"

She shook her head wretchedly. "I was *ten*, Daniel. We always had money. I never knew any other life. My mother told me it was my father's money. I accepted that. Why wouldn't I? When she remarried she married money. That was her way. I had part-time jobs all the time I was at university so I wouldn't be too much of a burden. I never thought Grandad was continuing to look out for us."

"Well he was," Berne said, sounding equally wretched.

"Your mother should have told you, Sandra," Daniel said. "She had a duty to tell you."

"Shameless bitch!" Berne muttered. "Never did tell the truth. All she was ever interested in was herself. Dad was right about her. You should think about it instead of blaming Dad."

"I love my mother, Berne," Sandra said, unable to disentangle herself from the ties that bind.

"Fine!" he fumed. "I know you can love someone and be disgusted with them at the same time. Why did Grandad bypass me for you? Sons and grandsons always have the inside track."

"I know they do," Sandra acknowledged. "Maybe Grandad knew I was the most likely to try to hold on to our inheritance. The Kingston inheritance. Kingstons are buried here, Berne. Do we walk away from Moondai and leave them here?"

Berne gave a strangled laugh. "They're *dead*, Sandra. They're gone forever. They don't know and they don't care."

"But *I* care," Sandra said. "I want to be loyal to my ancestors, to my dad and my grandfather, harsh though he was to us. I don't want to betray them."

"You're too young to be such a sentimental fool," Berne said in disgust. "The dead are dead. No way do they care about our actions. As for Daniel here—" he shot Daniel a glowering look "—he's a fast worker. I'm betting he was offered the deal of a lifetime on a silver platter. He gets Moondai but you're part of the package. He couldn't have imagined such a scenario in his wildest dreams. But a word of caution."

"Okay, let's hear it, Berne," Daniel clipped off,

looking like he was more than ready to hear it and deal with it if needs be.

"It's for my *cousin,* pal," Berne emphasized, predisposed to hating Daniel Carson for so many reasons; showing him up without even trying, relating so easily to his grandfather when Rigby Kingston had produced awe, fear and a great deal of anxiety in him and everyone else, and just to compound the problem, it appeared very much like Daniel had Sandra sold on him on sight. It tied Berne in knots and made him doubly aggressive. "We don't know anything much about you, do we, Dan?" he charged. "You're a dark horse if ever there was one. Grandad accepted you on the word of a fellow cattleman. So you did a good job in the Channel Country? I guess you've always been hell-bent on climbing the ladder. Personally I think you should be investigated. Most people have things to hide. We know nothing about your background for instance. Sandra should make it her business to find out."

But Sandra was reeling from Berne's disclosures. "You think Grandad didn't check Daniel out?" she asked, staring at her cousin.

Berne shrugged. "It was different with Grandad. No man had power over him, but from what I can see Daniel has power over *you* already."

"He must if you say so, Berne." She looked at her cousin with acute distaste. The charge stung like a whip because it was *true.*

"Look how you treat him for God's sake!" Berne wheeled a half circle in his rage. "You've installed him in the house. It would never have happened in Grandad's day. Dad certainly wouldn't have allowed it. Daniel is *staff*. He's got the overseer's bungalow. It's good enough for him."

Sandra noted the sharp shift in Daniel's lean powerful body. She moved to stand between them. If there was any physical confrontation she knew Berne would come off second best. "Let's say I want Daniel on call, Berne. Not a good distance away. Yesterday we crash landed in a crocodile infested swamp. Incredibly Daniel was able to bring the chopper down in a clearing the size of a bathtub. The sad thing is, it's my *family* I don't trust. There's a great deal at stake here. You and Uncle Lloyd did handsomely out of Grandad's will as you should, but you're filled with bitter resentments. I understand that. I got the lion's share. But I think most people in my position would find themselves with a few more fears than they started out with. I've made a judgment in regards Daniel. I've elected to trust him."

"More fool's you!" Berne's voice trembled with anger. "It's just as I said. He's got to you already. Just be careful, cousin. That's all I'm saying."

"What have *I* got to gain from something happening to Sandra, Berne?" Daniel asked in a voice that would have brought anyone up short.

"Not now. Not yet," Berne said obscurely, turning to go.

"If you've got concerns why don't you go to the authorities?" Daniel began to move towards him.

"Daniel, please." Sandra grasped his arm. "I will be careful, Berne. I don't need you to tell me. My mother has always believed the Cessna was sabotaged when Dad was flying it. That means someone got away with a crime." Even as she said it Sandra felt shame. Berne had had nothing to do with it even if he had been an awful kid, jealous, resentful, always spoiling for a fight.

"That's your stupid mother talking," Berne rasped, his tanned skin turning white. "You might have a little chat with her. You talk about untrustworthy? You can't go past her. Uncle Trevor wasn't supposed to make that trip anyway. It was Grandad." He punched the words out, turned on his heel and stomped off down the hall.

For a moment Sandra couldn't catch her breath. Confusion was growing at such a rate of intensity her mind was in turmoil. "Could that possibly be true?" she managed eventually. "Have you ever heard it?" Her legs felt so wobbly she had to sit down.

"Never." Daniel's voice was rough with concern. "And I've heard plenty of talk. Don't upset yourself, Sandra. You've gone very pale."

"Why would he say it?" She searched those silver-grey eyes.

"God knows." Daniel could see the shock in her. There were far too many revelations for her to handle all at once. "He's been making a lot of wild accusations."

"So that's it, wild accusations?"

He saw the doubts that brushed her expression. Doubts that made something flare deep in his eyes. "So who should you believe, Sandra?" he asked in a dead-serious voice. "Because it's *you* who has to decide."

CHAPTER SEVEN

IN THE days that followed Sandra had plenty of time to mull over Berne's revelations. Had it really been her grandfather and not her father who was to have flown to the Kingston outstation that fateful day? Her grandfather had long been accustomed to flying off on regular inspections, often without notice because he took pleasure in catching the staff on the hop. On numerous occasions he had taken her father along with him. As the heir apparent, her father was being groomed to one day take over the reins. Berne had sounded so *sure*. She struggled to understand how, if that were so, her mother had been able to maintain her silence.

She had lost no time ringing her mother in an effort to set the record straight. Just as she feared, immediately she broached the subject, her mother became highly emotional. That was Pam's way of protecting herself from being questioned too closely. Pam invariably resorted to controlled hysteria. She swore she knew nothing of the change of plan. When asked about where their money had come from after they left Moondai, she had flown into a fit of defensiveness saying she had never spoken to Sandra about financial matters because they simply weren't her concern. Whatever lines of credit Rigby Kingston had made available, it was his duty to do so. He was a hateful man. Pam was overjoyed he was dead. Sandra deserved everything that had come her way. Moondai would have gone to her father in any case. Sandra should not upset her like this. That part of her life as a Kingston was long over. Besides, Mickey had chicken pox and needed her attention.

All in all the phone call had been a stomach churning disaster. Her mother had even been crass enough to call her stepfather to the phone to say a few affectionate words, but Sandra had all but hurled the phone down, thinking though she loved her mother Pam was a fool. It made life so much easier if one didn't have to look truth in the face.

The upshot was Sandra felt desperate to get confirmation from her uncle. Daniel had urged her to do so, but somehow she always baulked at the last moment. If Berne's claim was true and not made up on the spur of the moment, it would open up an entirely new avenue of thought. Her grandfather had made enemies over the years. He had never been what one would call popular. In fact a lot of people wouldn't have been upset by his demise. But surely his son wouldn't have conspired against him? Her father had been without question, the favourite, but by no means had Rigby Kingston closed the door on his younger son. Though Lloyd's consuming interest in cataloguing the native flora had been a mystery and an irritation to his father, Lloyd had been allowed to make his numerous field trips and tour the country at will. They all lived in what most people would consider, splendour, all financed by Rigby Kingston, notoriously miserly in some areas and surprisingly generous in others.

Mystery piled on top of mystery. It was those closest to Sandra she felt she couldn't trust. Not even Elsa who lived on the periphery of everyone's attention. In some ways Elsa was like a resident ghost, forever hovering about without really being seen or heard. Whatever had happened to the handsome, hardworking, businesswoman of yesterday? Happiness had passed Elsa by. But what had actually happened to cause her to pass from one state to the other? Certainly her grandfather had been an autocratic man but one would have thought Elsa in her mid-forties when they married would have been able to cope with him? There must have been attraction between them for them to have married in the first place. Instead Elsa had turned into a watcher, not a doer as hollowed out inside as if she'd been gutted. That in itself was a mystery. The empty shell of her marriage was now over, but still

Elsa made no move to get on with a new and better life.

Sandra on the other hand made a good start on learning about the running of Moondai. As the weeks went by Daniel was able to spend more and more time with her though the amount of time was determined by his own heavy work schedule. She was grateful he was loosening up his routine in order to be able to show her the ropes. It had taken no time at all to discover his workload was considerable. He was on the job at sunup, not returning to the homestead until well after sunset. Consequently she never saw him at breakfast or lunch, meeting up maybe an hour before dinner when they retired to the office. There they read through piles of memos, invoices, letters and documents that Andy, the station accountant had arranged in batches for inspection and signature where necessary. Whatever decisions Daniel came to regarding the business side of running the station he explained the reasons for it, going into quite a bit of detail and not fobbing her off or treating her as if her opinion at this early stage had little value. He treated her like the intelligent person she was. She liked that about him. Her uncle invariably talked down to her. Sandra had never thought of herself as a businesswoman in the making, but she was finding learning about all these financial matters far more interesting than she ever supposed.

"Your grandfather has left you one of the finest

cattle stations in the country and the fortune to keep it intact," Daniel told her. "It's important you understood how everything works. You have a good mind. Now's a great opportunity to use it."

To that end she and Daniel continued their learning sessions for a couple of hours after dinner. Even dinner had turned into a routine with some degree of normalcy. Her uncle solved the problem of Daniel's presence at the table by addressing the odd civil remark to him but concentrating on his niece. Sandra who had no great knowledge of the desert flora but had always been filled with wonderment at the phenomenon of the vast desert gardens began to avail herself of her uncle's extensive knowledge.

"Don't start him off for God's sake!" Berne had warned when she first started to show an interest.

"You're incapable of appreciating the beauties of nature, Bernard," his father responded, finding he was warming to his niece now that she had become an adult. Sandra had been a very precocious little girl as he recalled. Something both his father and brother had encouraged no doubt to counter Pamela's single digit IQ.

But it was to Daniel Sandra always turned for advice and instruction. It was getting so she couldn't hide her feelings. From herself at least. She prided herself she had the sense not to allow Daniel to see how important he was to her. That might have put him in a very awkward position.

She knew she was more than half way in love with him—hell, madly in love with him—which might have been precisely what her grandfather had in mind. Just thinking about it all was interfering with her sleep and her thought processes. To counter her increasing need for him and his company she upped her businesslike manner. The last thing she wanted to do was put pressure on him. A girl had her pride. Daniel was there to give her protection, to be her friend and mentor, so that when his year was up she could step into his shoes albeit with the help of a professional station manager they would select together.

End of story or the start of a great adventure?

It was only when she lay in bed at night, thinking about him, she wondered if he were fooled by the briskness of her manner. She was so *aware* of him, every word he spoke, every inflection, the way he laughed, the way he walked, the gleaming glances he sent in her direction, every gesture he made. When their hands brushed, whilst passing documents to one another, little electric shocks zapped through her. There was such a *buzz* around him. No use pretending. She was in *deep*. It amazed and alarmed her, causing her to wonder if her own susceptibility had overtones of her mother? She had seen too much of vulnerable women. She had no intention of becoming one.

* * *

It took six weeks before they received a full report on the helicopter crash.

Daniel stood by the window in the study reading it, a frown of concentration between his brows.

"Well?" Sandra couldn't stand the suspense.

He broke off to look at her. "Nothing much new."

"Damn, are you sure?"

He shoved that errant lock of hair off his forehead. "Of course I'm sure. You can read it in a minute. It's much the same as the preliminary report. Mechanical failure. There's no blame laid, no criticism of the maintenance of the aircraft. In fact a little pat on the back for me for pilot skills."

"Is that all they came up with?" Sandra felt angry and frustrated.

He sighed. "Don't get upset. We survived. The failure of mechanical components is well documented, Sandra. Now we have the chopper back, I'll have the hangar, attended by day and locked up at night. It's never been done before."

"So we drop the whole thing?" Sandra showed her dissatisfaction.

"Nothing else we can do." Daniel shrugged in acceptance. Nevertheless he quietly went about putting new security measures in place.

It didn't take long for a steady stream of visitors to start to call; station people and business people from Alice Springs who wanted to welcome Rigby

Kingston's granddaughter back home. Most were good-hearted, Outback people simply wanting to wish her well. A few busybodies came to size her up. Gossip was rife Moondai might very well come onto the market. The wheeler-dealers wanted to be there on the ground floor. Even would-be suitors came to call; some overconfident, dressed nattily, some afflicted by stammering shyness that was painful to behold. None of them fortune hunters exactly—they were all from established families—but young men looking for a suitable wife and future mother for their brood. Sandra's enviable financial standing made her a prize candidate.

The consensus of opinion was made available by way of the grapevine. Alexandra Kingston would make some lucky bloke the perfect wife.

"The word's gone out," Daniel told her, a dry note in his voice. They were sitting atop a fence watching a mob of around thirty brumbies being drafted. For wild horses they had surprisingly well developed muscles and came in varied colours, bay, iron grey, black, big, medium, compact sized, some showing station blood. One liver chestnut beauty was trying its level best to bite a stockman on the shoulder.

"What word?" She turned on him so precipitously he had to grab her to prevent her falling.

"Why your beauty of course, Ms Kingston." His eyes beneath the brim of his hat mocked her.

"And you're the expert?" she asked tartly, to cover

the strain of sitting next to him without being able to touch him. Every single day she was reacting more *bodily* to him. Lord help her she wanted him to crush her in his arms. Envelop her. A great thing had happened to her. She was head over heels in love. Then there was the other thing which might or might not have significance but she had to find out from him.

Among the visitors who wished to renew their acquaintance were station people called McAuliffe accompanied by their only daughter, Alanna. Sandra vaguely remembered Alanna, although Alanna was several years older, a vibrantly attractive brunette with a shapely figure and unusual coffee-coloured eyes.

Memories of that afternoon kept coming… After partaking of afternoon tea and complementing Meg on her cooking, Alanna stood up with an appealing, "Do you mind if I go off and find Daniel?"

Sandra had been shocked at her own reaction. She'd wanted to tell Alanna to back the hell off. She was *jealous,* when she had vowed never, never to become a jealous woman.

"I need him to confirm something," Alanna explained. "Would you mind if I borrow the Jeep?" she asked prettily, casting her eyes over the Jeep that Sandra kept parked in the drive for her own use.

Again Sandra couldn't for the life of her wring out a "Please do."

"There's a ball coming up." Alanna looked back,

big eyed. "Daniel has promised to be my partner. He's just so much in demand, I'm thrilled out of my mind it's going to be me."

"Lana's absolutely *crazy* about him," Mrs. McAuliffe piped up, just in case Sandra had missed the message. "Daniel's enormously popular with the girls. There's something about him that makes the knees buckle," she gushed, turning quite pink cheeked herself.

"We're kinda hoping something good might come of it," Mr. McAuliffe tacked on, cracking his knuckles.

Over my dead body!

"Prickly little thing aren't you," Daniel interrupted her recollections, amused by her feisty expression. "It just so happens I *like* it. You must have known you were going to attract every last bachelor from eighteen to eighty in the Territory and beyond."

"I'm relying on you to put it about I'm very bad-tempered," she said shortly.

She had taken off her akubra and damp golden curls clung to her nape. Her hair had grown so quickly Daniel thought, resisting the powerful urge to fluff the gilded halo that had replace the short petalled look. No wonder the little kids at the hospital had mistaken her for an angel. But she was more spicy than sweet though she had her sweet moments. A man couldn't ask for more he thought. But it wasn't going to happen to him.

Forget it, Daniel.

The words dropped as dull as stones.

"Unfortunately temper doesn't put a man off," he said. "It's the really *nice* girls who tend to get overlooked."

"That certainly doesn't apply to your friend Alanna," Sandra retorted, sharper than she meant. *Be careful. Be careful. Don't give yourself away.* "Now there's a sexpot if ever I've seen one. Are you going to the ball with her?"

He laughed, an infinitely attractive sound to her ears. "Though tempted I had to turn her down."

She turned her head to stare at him. He was worth staring at. He had a beautifully structured chin and jawline. She wanted to trace it with her hand. She was painfully aware of the excitement that was throbbing inside her, wishing and wishing she could pass her excitement on to him. "She told me you had *promised*. I'm surprised at you, Daniel. You shouldn't break a promise."

"As it happened, I didn't." He whistled at a hostile horse with a star-shaped white blaze on its forehead. The horse amazingly quietened, ears tipped forward. "Alanna thinks if she wants something badly enough she'll get it."

"And she wants you. Mamma and Poppa made that clear. You better remind her you're working for *me*."

"Yes, Ms Kingston." He tipped a tanned finger, eyes sparkling. "Anyway what's not to want?" he quipped.

"I suppose. You're very likeable, Daniel," she said

kindly. "What are you going to do with your life? You're so clever and capable."

"You forgot popular." His glance seemed to mock her. "Trying to get rid of me already?"

She wanted to say, you can stay forever but was worried about frightening him off. How could you stop yourself from giving your heart away? It just happened. "The truth is I'm coming to rely on you more and more, Daniel," she said. "Do you suppose— I don't want you to take this the wrong way—but do you suppose Grandad had some master plan in mind?"

Sunlight made a dazzle of his eyes. "For you and me?"

His tone was so highly sceptical she was stopped in her tracks. "Well we all know it wouldn't work. I am resolved not to get married anyway. But I keep wondering why he arranged things the way he did. Berne stirred things up as he meant to. There's got to be some logic to it. Grandad was nothing if not logical. Did he assume in throwing the two of us together some magic might happen? Or more likely did he think we'd see it in materialistic terms? What would undoubtedly advantage you would advantage me as you could successfully step straight into Grandad's shoes. You'd maintain authority and style. You said yourself it made a kind of sense."

His mouth twisted. "Where would I get style from, Sandra?" he asked as though he was burdened by some terrible legacy. "I have no family, not a lot of money but enough to get started somewhere on my own and I didn't get to go to university, like you. But a good man made sure I got the benefit of a fair education. He would have let me continue but I was too determined to pay him back."

"That was Harry Cunningham from the Channel Country?" she asked with care.

"You've done your homework. What else have you found out about me?" His tone was astonishingly clipped.

"Don't get mad. It was Vince Taylor who told me," she said, trying to sound casual when she'd really been pumping foreman Vince, for information. "Mr. Cunningham must have been a good man."

"The best," Daniel confirmed.

"Obviously. He trained you. As for style, as far as I'm concerned, style is innate. It's knowing who *you* are, not who your dad was; what *you* are. You've got good blood in you, Daniel."

"The hell I have!" It came out like a soft growl.

"Oh, you've got good blood all right," she insisted. "You'd be at home anywhere."

He gave her a smouldering glance. "Your family doesn't seem to think so. I'd be lucky if your appalling snob of an uncle addresses two words to me over dinner."

"I wouldn't have a nervous breakdown about it," she said dryly. "Uncle Lloyd is worried *you'll* ask him something he doesn't know. Think about it. Exactly what does he know about? He's spent his whole life on Moondai but he couldn't possibly run it. His towering achievement is becoming an amateur botanist."

"Well that in itself is something," Daniel said with unexpected approval, given Lloyd Kingston's patronising manner with him. "I'm like you I'm finding the whole area fascinating. I've even taken to looking out for the exquisite little plants tucked away in the canyons. Botany is a legitimate career. Your uncle would have been a much happier man had he struck out for himself. The same goes for Berne."

"It hasn't occurred to you both of them are bone lazy?" Sandra said, marvelling that it was so.

"Now that you mention it, yes. Listen, much as I'm enjoying the break, I must go. I have to do some bull catching this afternoon with a couple of the men. The tallest and the fittest."

"So they can lift the steel panels for the portable yards?"

"Right on." He gave her a little nod of approval. "You might only have been ten when you left but you haven't forgotten much. It's great you've kept up your riding, too." She was, in fact, a natural born horsewoman. He took great pleasure in watching her ride, knowing she loved horses as much as he did.

Daniel swung himself off the fence in one lithe movement, without thinking, holding up his arms for her.

Yes, yes! She craved those strong arms around her, those tanned hands holding her, his hard muscled chest against her cheek.

"Catch me!" she invited, joyous as a child. She threw out her own arms launching her feather light body at him.

But it wasn't a child who landed in his arms. It was a woman who was growing more lovely, more sexually exciting by the day. Just holding her was dangerous. Her skin was perfection even in the strong sunlight. Her buttery curls swept up from her graceful neck. Her full tender lips were curved in a smile but it was her eyes that drew Daniel in. So deep and so sparkling a blue he wanted to drown in their lagoon-like depths.

A woman's beauty and sexual allure was a powerful weapon to render a man helpless. A weapon he couldn't risk putting into her hands. There was no way he could reverse their station in life. She was the Kingston heiress; he was the overseer. He had to hold tight to his pride though he realised had they been on their own and stockmen weren't around, all it would have taken was to tighten his hold on her and lower his head.

Desire swept through Daniel's body like a dark rushing river. He couldn't step back from it. It was

on him. All of his senses were astonishingly *keen.*
Sight. Sound. Smell. Touch. They were far too close,
their heads bent to one another, both of them seemingly fearing to speak. He could savour the fresh
scent of her; feel the heat off her body. She was the
very essence of femininity. He could almost *taste*
her on his palate.

For one long precious moment he allowed himself
to be held in thrall. He couldn't even think straight;
just standing there, holding her, drenched in a
yearning so powerful, so evocative of something
just beyond his reach, it was causing him *pain.* He
wondered with an unfamiliar surge of panic what
more lay in store for him. What could happen from
this point on? This was no fleeting attraction. It was
something over which he was losing control. Yet
getting her to fall in love with *him* wouldn't be so
difficult. He had enough experience to recognise
that. He could see the little electric flame in her
eyes. What burned her burned him.

Only it wasn't *right.* This was far more than a mo-
mentary indiscretion; it was as good as forbidden.
She was quite alone. Her family wasn't much use to
her. She relied on him; she trusted him. Sometimes
she seemed *so terrifyingly* young and innocent. He
couldn't possibly hurt her or betray that innocence
which he knew instinctively she retained for all that
predatory stepfather who deserved to be pummelled
into the ground.

Daniel made his decision. Falling in love was not only a powerful emotion, it could come as a body blow. One false move could spoil everything. They were friends. They could never be lovers. He stepped back abruptly, dropping his arms.

"I do believe you've put on six or seven kilos?" He rallied sufficiently to make a joke.

"I'll be a butterball in no time," she said, herself faring quite well in regaining her balance. As he turned away she called, "Do you think you could spare me a full hour tomorrow, Daniel?"

"Sure, what for?" He stood in a characteristic pose with his two hands on his lean hips, long fingers pointing down.

She took immense pleasure in his dynamic male aura. "I want to learn how to ride a motorbike," she told him with feigned casualness.

His expression was comical. She might just as well have said she wanted to learn to drive the bulldozer and start ripping up new tracks for the road trains. "Is that a good idea?" He couldn't bear the idea of her coming off a bike, even a minor spill could break bones though he knew her look of fragility was deceptive. She was actually quite strong.

"Heck, Daniel, we're in the middle of nowhere," she protested. "You can show me, can't you or will I get Chris to show me?" She knew she was provoking him. Chris Barrett was a good-looking, full of himself, young jackeroo who was doing a year's stint on the station before taking up a position in the family engineering firm in Brisbane. Hugely enjoying his gap year Chris flirted openly with her though the older stockmen were at pains to make clear to him he was crossing the line.

"Just let's forget Chris," Daniel said dryly. "As a rider I don't regard him very highly, let alone as a teacher. Your grandfather only took him on as a favour to his family. He'll never make a cattleman not that he was ever meant to. Please don't give him any encouragement. He's impudent enough as it is." But harmless, Daniel knew, otherwise he'd have been told to pack up his gear and leave.

"I've forgotten him already," Sandra said airily. "So I can count on an hour tomorrow?"

"Okay," he nodded briskly.

"I'd like to be able to handle the dozer." She kept a perfectly straight face as she said it.

"Forget the dozer," he said, firmly. "It's by no means easy to operate, weighing in as it does at around thirty-eight tons. There's a small tractor I'll let you have a go on one of these days."

"Thank you, Daniel." She gave him a radiant smile. "I've got a lot of learning in front of me. I want to be able to fly the Beech Baron and the helicopter in time."

His answer was serious which greatly pleased her. "Flying lessons can be arranged," he said. "I thought you *hated* flying?"

"So I do and why wouldn't I?" she retorted. "But

it was wonderful up there with you in the chopper before we crashed. The best way to get over my fears might well be to learn how to fly. Don't you think?" She tipped her head to one side, staring at him, trying to understand this momentous thing that was happening between them.

He nodded his agreement. "It's the only way to get around. I know a very patient and competent teacher."

"You?" she asked hopefully.

He shook his head. "Not me. I'd find that too nerve-racking." He softened it with a smile. "This guy, Paddy Hyland runs the Hyland School of Aviation at the Alice. He's very good, gently spoken and he has the patience of Job."

"So what are you saying, females need to be mollycoddled?"

"Well gentleness makes women feel better, Sandra."

"Plus females need instructors with the patience of Job?"

"Now you're starting to get the hang of it." That engaging dimple flickered in his cheek.

"Have you failed to notice how smart I am, Daniel?"

"Sandra, I haven't failed to notice every last little thing about you," he said with such a note in his voice it turned her insides out. "Have a nice day now!" He sketched a salute. "I'll see you tonight."

Make that every night of our lives!

CHAPTER EIGHT

SANDRA had been going steadily through paperwork since around nine o'clock that morning. It was now eleven and Meg came to the door with a cup of coffee and a freshly baked apple and cinnamon muffin. She stopped for a while chatting—Meg was always cheerful—then went on her way. Sandra had insisted Meg get more help in running the house—it was so big. Elsa did nothing to lend a hand so far as Sandra could see—so Meg had taken two young aboriginal girls under her wing for training. Sandra often heard their infectious laughter issuing from the kitchen and around the house. It brightened up the atmosphere and she was glad of it.

Elsa kept mostly to her suite of rooms—she had not shared a bedroom with Sandra's grandfather for many years—or she took her long rambling walks. The family cemetery was one of her haunts though she hadn't taken to laying flowering branches on her husband's grave as Sandra often did at the grave of her father. In fact Sandra had given instructions for a number of advanced white bauhinias to be planted around the perimeter which was guarded by a tall wrought iron fence. Immensely hardy the bauhinias would lend shade and their loveliness to that desolate place. It had been kept in perfect order but an aura of melancholy hung over it. She finished what she was doing, put her signature to the crosses Daniel had marked for her, then decided on the spur of the moment to ride out to the family plot to check on the new plantings. The worst of the heat was over and the desert days sparkled.

On her way she stopped to break off several long branches of the fluffy flowered pink mulla-mulla, a desert ephemeral that threw a blushing veil over the landscape. Some of the branches stood as tall as herself as did the desert grevillea which was one of the most spectacular flowering trees of the Red Centre.

Most of her friends from her student days thought the desert extremely arid, a terrifying, life threatening place, which of course it was under certain circumstances. What they didn't appear to know or had never seen was the desert after the rains; a wonderland on such a scale it made the most beautiful of city gardens, even the botanical gardens, look pocket handkerchief-sized by comparison. What large country garden for that matter ran to the horizon? Where else were there carpets of white, yellow and pink everlastings covering fifty square miles? Her home, Moondai, was a world apart. She had already resolved to hold on to it. Her ancestors lay buried in the lava-red earth.

When she reached the cemetery she slipped off her horse, a highly responsive mare, and tethered it to a branch of an old gum. The gum was almost a sculpture, gnarled and twisted in its endless struggle against the harshness of sun and wind. A short distance away was the iron fenced enclosure with its marble and granite headstones. No one to disturb you here, she thought a melancholy shiver running down her spine.

A great flock of budgerigar, the phenomenon of the Inland, winged overhead drawing her eyes. They were flying in their curious V formation seeking out the nearest water which was maybe half a mile off at Jirra Jarra Creek, its banks graced by a magnificent corridor of red river gums. She took a few moments to watch the squadron of little birds flame across the sky, emerald green and gold, the colours of the nation, then she gathered the mass of pink flowers Outback people called "lamb's tails" and strode off. Once inside the massive gate she noted with satisfaction the bauhinias had responded well to their new home. She had expected to see one or two wilting but they showed their toughness holding their silvery green foliage aloft. Their seasonal flowering was over but come September-October they should be out in all their shining white glory. She had always loved the bauhinias as a child; the pink, the white, the purple, cerise. The aboriginals believed they were spirit people. It was a good idea to have them encircle this place where the bones of so many generations of Kingstons lay.

Carefully Sandra paid her respects to her grandfather and the grandmother, Catherine, she had never known, then moved on to the grave of her father, speaking aloud to him as she had as a child. His had been a bittersweet marriage—her mother had never settled in her desert home—but she had always understood her father had deeply loved her, his only child. The happiness and security of her childhood had been destroyed by his death. Her mother, even now, had not apologised for saying her husband's own brother had had something to do with it. She stuck to her claim that Lloyd Kingston was *evil* but though Sandra kept her uncle under constant close observation she couldn't see it. In fact it was starting to seem *unthinkable*. Perhaps her mother had wanted revenge for her brother-in-law's harsh criticism of her own lifestyle? Whatever the reason her uncle should never have used her, a child, as a weapon in their war. *That* had been truly unforgivable even if at some stage he'd believed his claim she wasn't a Kingston. It had only recently struck her, her uncle and her cousin had laboured all their lives for her grandfather's love and approval without ever getting it. Small wonder it had caused such bitterness and driven a wedge between them and *her*. The great irony was the grandfather who had banished her had made her his heir. Should anything happen to her, her uncle Lloyd would inherit the entire estate.

Daniel found her an hour later, sitting in solitude on a stone bench. He tethered his horse beside the mare, watching the animals acknowledge each other with companionable whinnies, before walking towards the enclosure.

"Sandra," he called gently.

She lifted her sunny head that always reminded him of a lovely flower on a stalk, holding up a hand.

How do I withstand her? he asked himself, unnerved at the speed with which she had gotten not only under his skin but right into the deepest cavern of his heart. Sandra Kingston was a dream he had been hankering after all his life. She was also, like a dream, out of reach.

Close to, he could see the track of tears on her satin cheeks. He was deeply moved, thinking he would always hold that little picture of her sitting here, weeping gentle tears.

"Hi, come sit beside me," she invited, moving along the bench a little so he would have room.

"I feel I'm intruding," he commented, his eyes on her poignant profile.

"No, you're not." She gave him a reassuring smile. "I was talking to Dad."

"Does he ever answer?" He yanked off his hat, relishing the cooling breeze on his head.

"Sometimes." She dashed the back of her hand over her eyes. "There's so much I'm desperate to know, Daniel. Living with my unhappy family these past months I just can't believe Uncle Lloyd had anything to do with Dad's death."

"I've *never* believed it." Daniel's eyes rested on her floral offering, his own wounded heart contracting. "Apart from anything else, he just doesn't have it in him to take any sort of violent action. As I see it, your mother was expelled from the family home in disgrace. She retaliated by accusing your uncle of a heinous crime. She would have been shattered at the time. Your uncle had poured endless scorn on her. There's a limit to what people can take."

"So it *was* an accident?" she asked with a profound sigh.

"That was the result of the inquiry."

"So I've spent more than half my life believing a terrible lie?" Her blue eyes sought his.

"Some people use up *all* their life believing lies, Sandra."

"And our accident in the chopper? You had your suspicions, Daniel?" she reminded him. These moments they spent alone were becoming oddly intense as though it wasn't permitted for them to become too intimate.

He shrugged, not wanting to increase her sense of

hidden threat. "It just seemed like one accident too many. I jumped to conclusions."

"You don't sound too sure?" She watched his face, wanting to turn his chin a little towards her so she could stare into his eyes.

"Money creates an environment of suspicion, Sandra. In your case a great deal of money."

I've got money for both of us, she cried out inside but couldn't possibly say it aloud. Daniel was fiercely independent and proud.

"Money and passions coexist," he continued. "Anger, bitterness, resentment, shameful, violent thoughts."

"So it would serve my family's ambitions if I didn't get to celebrate my twenty-first birthday?" she asked bleakly.

"Which is fast approaching." He traced the perfect oval of her face with his eyes. She had put a little weight on her fragile frame. It was immensely becoming, the woman emerging clearly from the young girl. "I'll have to start thinking of a present. By the way I have to fly to Darwin, this coming Friday. Joel Moreland wants to meet me."

That name beat against Sandra's brain. "Joel Moreland, the man with the Midas touch? You're not going to leave me for him, are you?" she asked, reduced to near panic.

"Hey, he only wants to meet me, Sandra." For a breathless second he almost pulled her into his arms to comfort her. "A man called Bill Morrissey set it up. He's a member of the Northern Territory Administration."

"Yes, I know. I've read about him," Sandra said, dismissing Morrissey. "So *why* does a man like Moreland want to meet you, Daniel, unless it's to offer you a job?" Her voice was unsteady with emotion.

"If he does, he does." Daniel shook his head, struggling to retain his own role of employee, friend and mentor. "I have to think of my future, Sandra. Let's face it by the time my year's up, you could either decide to sell Moondai or find yourself engaged to one of the drove of guys who've been calling. Don't for a moment think they haven't got their eye on Moondai as well as the fair maiden."

"Thank you, Daniel," she said crisply, tilting her delicately determined chin.

"Sandra, I've no wish to offend you. As lovable as you undoubtedly are, your rich inheritance would only make them love you more."

"You've made your point," she said acidly. "Or am I supposed to feel flattered they might want *me* at all?"

His mobile mouth twisted. "I just want you to be fully aware of the disadvantages of being an heiress."

"Don't worry. I'll have the lucky man vetted by you."

It distressed him just to hear her say it even in mockery. He locked his strong muscular arms behind his head. "What I started out to say was would you like to come along for the ride? I don't expect to be more than a couple of hours over lunch. You could do some shopping; visit an art gallery. We could meet up later. Actually I'd like you to meet Moreland. It's very handy to know a man like that. He could be a big help to you in the future."

"Well I'll need it, won't I with you planning to pack up and leave," Sandra burst out, startled by her impulse to throw herself into his arms and beg him to stay.

"What did you think was going to happen?" He turned on her, on the surface calm, underneath battling his own complicated needs and wants. Sandra Kingston coming into his life had exposed him to new and overwhelming emotions. Falling in love was the last thing he had seen coming.

"Oh, I don't know," she said. "The two of us surviving that crash entrenched you in my mind as a friend and protector, not just Moondai's overseer which you're determined to be."

"Well that's my job, Sandra," he said tersely. "We're both aware of that. We inhabit different worlds."

"We inhabit the *same* world!" She levelled him with an electric blue stare.

"Don't, Sandra," he said, deliberately using his position as employee as a shield.

Her cheeks flushed with anger. "Don't what?"

"Don't go where you're going."

She jumped up, a small fury, blazingly blue eyes smarting with her own lie. "I have no idea what you mean."

"I think you do."

"And you've decided to put me in my place?" she asked raggedly.

"That wasn't my aim." He stood up quiet, but commanding. "What I'm saying is I've decided to remain in *my* place."

"You have a hide!" Her voice trembled. He towered over her with those long legs but for once she didn't find it comforting.

"I'm sorry. You *must* understand."

"Well I don't!" Her vision was blurring with tears. She felt sick to the stomach; ashamed, humiliated. Furiously she blinked the tears away.

Daniel felt his heartbeats thudding like hammers. He was trying so hard to do the right thing. Did she know how much discipline that took? She couldn't, because it was her tears that tore at him and pushed him over the edge.

One moment he was standing stalwart, battling to suppress the emotions that were devouring him, the next he had hauled her headlong into his arms, his blood glittering, passion gripping him like a vise.

He took her mouth hungrily, his arms imprisoning rather than enfolding her. He was smothering her, he thought desperately, perhaps bruising her for days to come but he couldn't seem to loosen his hold much less let her go. Here was beauty, softness, sweetness he had never known. The perfect prize he could never win. His hands began to range over her body, down her back…smoothing, caressing. He had to stay them but his burning desire to know her body was driving him on.

A kiss, one kiss was never enough, but so *precious* because he might never get to kiss her again. He could feel his groin flood with blood, feeding a need so powerful it scared him. What might it feel like to surrender to such desire? To let the force of his passion for her sweep him away?

Her little moans fell audibly on his ears…little expiring breaths. He took it as she was *begging* him to release her. She had placed her hands upon his chest, powerless to push him away.

Immediately Daniel came to himself, afraid of his own strength.

"Sandra, I'm sorry. And in such a place!" With near superhuman control he drew back, setting her free. "Now you know me for what I am. A man like any other."

She shook her head, quite unable to speak. She was stunned by what had passed between them. It had far exceeded even her imagining. When she spoke, her voice was a husky murmur. "I provoked you, Daniel." She brought up her blue-violet eyes.

"I tried to warn you of what might happen." His body was throbbing painfully with denial.

"Do you fear it?"

"I wouldn't do anything in this world to hurt you," he said, his expression strained.

"I know that. But you're so high minded you won't let yourself be attracted to me, will you, Daniel?"

"I *can't* be. You know that." Daniel tried to rein in a sudden impotent anger, a railing against the world.

She threw out her arm. "So all this bothers you? Moondai, my money?"

"It's a pretty dazzling legacy, Sandra," he rasped. "You'd have to be one of the richest young women in the country."

"So my inheritance stands between us?" She too was struggling for composure.

"I'm not the man who can ignore it, Sandra. You're so young. There's much for you to see and do. You'll meet plenty of guys. Guys with fine respectable backgrounds. The right man you can trust to stand alongside you, with the strength to help you keep Moondai for yourself and your heirs. You only have to give yourself time."

"And you're *not* respectable, Daniel?" She gave a laugh of sorts.

He sighed deeply. "Of course I am as far as it goes. If you were an ordinary girl…"

"You'd do what?" Sandra challenged, raising her arched brows.

"Let's face it. You're *not!*"

"What if I gave my fortune away?"

"That is totally out of the question," he said with a fierce frown. "Your grandfather gave you the responsibility of holding on to Moondai. He knew you better than you know yourself, because you do *want* it, don't you?"

"I don't want it if it means losing you, Daniel," she said. There, for good or bad, she had come out with the simple truth. Daniel had invested her life with real meaning.

For an instant Daniel was seized by a feeling of joy that carried him right up high. Up, up into the wild blue yonder. Then he fell heavily to earth again with a pronounced thud. All he could do was ram his hands into his jeans pockets lest he reach for her again. "I shouldn't have kissed you," he said as though he took shame in his own weakness.

"I know," she agreed wryly, "because now I'm absolutely *sure.*"

He raised a hand as if to refute it. "You're not sure of anything, Sandra. God almighty, you're not even twenty-one. Maybe *any* guy could have kissed you."

She breathed a great sigh of frustration. "I'm going to forget you said that, Daniel. I might still be a virgin—and that's a little secret between the two of us—but let me tell you I've been kissed plenty of times. The earth didn't move. It moved a few minutes ago."

It was more like an earthquake for him, but he

wasn't at liberty to tell her. He was trying to guide her, not take advantage of her. "All the more reason to slow down, Sandra," he advised. "You need to give yourself time."

When I know right now.

A wry little smile formed on Sandra's mouth. She turned away from him. "You're not going to leave me until your year is up?"

"I'm bound over not to," he replied. "I wouldn't in any case until you felt you were ready. I want the best for you, Sandra."

"But you'd think about it if Joel Moreland made you some kind of offer?" She swung back to face him.

"I don't know *why* he wants to meet me, Sandra."

"Come off it," she said shortly. "You don't have to be too modest. Obviously he's heard good things about you. Every visitor who comes here has nothing *but* good things to say about you. You turned Harry Cunningham's station around. Grandad who was as tough as they come held you in high regard. You're not a *nobody,* Daniel."

"I'm not a fortune hunter, either," he said bluntly.

"Ah, the root of the problem!" She sighed. "You think if you and I grew closer people would think you were?"

He gave her a straight look. "Of course they would."

"No need to sound so outraged." She feigned non-chalance, deciding the smart thing to do was to cloak her emotions from now on in instead of emblazoning them on her sleeve. "All right, Daniel. I can see the wisdom of what you're saying. I'm going to take your advice. I'm going to give myself plenty of time to meet lots of eligible guys. Establishment families of course, stuffy old money, reeking arrogance like Berne. The right blood lines are important apparently. No others need apply. And I *would* like to go along for the ride to Darwin. You can introduce me to Joel Moreland while you're at it. Okay?"

His eyes distant he leaned forward and picked up his akubra shoving it on his head as though he had a dozen pressing reasons to be on his way. "Whatever you say, Ms Kingston."

It was a major shock for Daniel to meet Joel Moreland. For one thing Moreland seemed *familiar* which Daniel didn't think had all that much to do with the fact Moreland regularly got his picture in the papers. It was more a real *frisson* as though he'd met up with someone he'd known in another lifetime. Moreland too seemed overtaken by the same force. He put out his hand with a charming smile, but his eyes behind his dark framed glasses had an intensity far beyond mere interest. "I thought we should meet, Daniel."

"Good to meet *you,* sir." Daniel shook the outstretched hand, responding to the warmth and firmness of Moreland's grip.

"Let's go straight into the dining room shall

we?" Bill Morrissey suggested, himself looking faintly puzzled.

What was this really all about, Daniel wondered, aware Moreland kept looking at him as they walked to their table. Joel Moreland was a splendid looking man. In his early seventies he was even more impressive in the flesh than in his photographs. Over six feet tall, he had a full head of silver hair and classic features that looked eminently trustworthy. His accent was cultured. He dressed with casual elegance. He looked what he was, a dignified man of real consequence.

Although his interests were huge Daniel was soon to discover Moreland had no hint of elitism or arrogance about him. It wasn't his reputation in any case. He put Daniel in mind of a wise elder statesman, even a revered grandfather, kindly and genial but Daniel couldn't fail to miss the high level of concentration that was being levelled at him. What was it all about? He wasn't a candidate for high political office with Moreland the backer.

Lunch, however, started out well and continued in that vein. Moreland and Morrissey were friends over many years, each comfortable in the other's company. The conversation ranged over a wide number of topics: became focused on the areas of importance to the Northern Territory, its economy and its future. Moondai worked its way into the discussion; Alexandra Kingston's unexpected inheritance over her uncle and cousin, Daniel's position as her overseer.

"She doesn't want to sell then?" Moreland asked, his eyes keen.

"Why, sir, are you interested?" Daniel met the inquiry head on.

Moreland smiled. "As a matter of fact, Daniel, I'm delighted to hear Ms Kingston wants to hold on to her heritage. I knew her grandfather of course and the whole sorry business. It was a tragedy about Trevor. He and my own son were actually friends. Both gone now leaving their families bereft. Rigby changed a great deal after he lost Trevor. He became very bitter. As for his young granddaughter, I'm looking forward to meeting her." Daniel had already mentioned Sandra was in Darwin and had expressed the desire to meet Joel Moreland which seemed to please this great man.

Bill Morrissey excused himself after the main course, having told them he had an important meeting with a Federal Minister, leaving Daniel and Joel Moreland alone.

If it's coming, it's coming now, Daniel thought. An offer of some kind. He'd be a fool if he hadn't cottoned on to the fact Joel Moreland was extraordinarily interested in him. In fact Moreland did nothing to disguise it. It was very flattering and almost but not quite, alarming. Their personalities seemed to be in too much harmony.

"I'm unsure how to begin, Daniel," Moreland said, sounding oddly uncertain for him.

"I find that hard to believe, sir," Daniel commented. What could Moreland possibly say that could cause a moment's awkwardness?

"Do you know why I wanted to see you? Lord knows I've heard enough about you."

"To perhaps offer me a job?" Daniel flashed his engaging smile.

"I'd offer you a job tomorrow, Daniel," Moreland replied. "But that's not the reason. I'm looking into your background."

Instantly the smile was wiped from Daniel's face. "I don't exactly have a background, Mr. Moreland," he said, wondering if the meeting was going to end right there. "My mother is dead. I have no idea who my father was. I know one usually knows but my mother couldn't bring herself to tell me."

"Don't upset yourself, son." Surprisingly Moreland put out a large hand, tapping Daniel's reassuringly much like a father figure. "I know the terrible thing that was done to you and your mother. However, I believe there might be a connection with *my* family."

Daniel's silver eyes flashed as though Moreland had made a cruel joke. "That's not possible, sir, I'm sorry."

"Nevertheless I've been looking into it," Moreland said, a discernible tremble in his self-assured voice.

"So this is what it's all about?"

Moreland looked down at his linked hands. "Sometimes guilt or the perception of guilt can cling to the innocent. It's only recently been suggested to me my son may have fathered a child. Imagine the shock, Daniel! I had great difficulty taking it in. I thought I knew everything there was to know about my wife but my sister-in-law tells me otherwise."

Daniel's eyes were like ice. "Why would she wait to tell you now? Forgive me, sir, but your son has been dead for many long years."

"Twenty-eight and I've grieved for every day of it," Moreland said heavily. "My wife died eight months ago. She never got over the loss of our boy. I have a daughter and a beautiful granddaughter, Cecile. They live in Melbourne. They visit me on all the right occasions but I have no one who can step into my shoes. That was Jared's role. Rigby and I always thought there was a parallel. I lost Jared. He lost Trevor. There's Lloyd, I know and Lloyd's boy. Rigby had grave misgivings about leaving Moondai to them."

"He spoke to you about it?" Daniel couldn't keep the shock from his voice.

Moreland nodded. "There was no great friendship between us. Rigby wasn't an easy man to know or like but there was a bond. All he could think of was a way to keep Moondai going."

Daniel sat back in his chair looking highly wary. "I hope the plan didn't involve *me*."

Moreland spread his hands. "Who knows? Having said that most would agree his young granddaughter couldn't possibly run it without a good man by her side. Young as you are, you managed to win Rigby's respect. No mean feat. He spoke at length about you on the last occasion I saw him which was shortly before he died. I would have been at his funeral only I was in Beijing at the time as part of a trade mission."

"So what did you read into it, Mr. Moreland, if I dare ask?"

Moreland searched Daniel's eyes. "That his granddaughter had to marry well. I'm not talking money here. I'm talking marrying a man eminently suitable to take over the running of Moondai."

"Well there's a sort of logic about it," Daniel said, his attractive voice turned unnaturally hard, "but like all things hard to pull off. For one thing it's not the sort of thing *I* would be party to."

"You mean marry a woman to take a giant leap up in life and control of one of our finest cattle stations?"

Daniel counted to twenty before replying. "That's exactly what I mean. I'm no fortune hunter."

"I can see that you're not, Daniel," Moreland spoke soothingly. "But the Kingstons aside, I want you to look at this." He reached into the breast pocket of his linen jacket and extracted a photograph which he handed to Daniel. "Do you know this young woman?"

"Should I?" Daniel's brows knit.

"Have a look."

Daniel took the photograph into his hand, staring down at the young woman's face. For a moment he almost gave way to anger. This wasn't happening. Why was Moreland doing this? Clearly he too was distressed. That fact alone made Daniel get a grip on himself. "What is this?" he asked in a tight voice. "Some skeleton in the cupboard you've let out? This is a photograph of my mother when she was young. The eyes are unmistakable." Large, beautiful dark eyes filled with more sadness than laughter.

"And her name was?" Moreland persisted, his fine face creased with emotion.

Daniel forced himself to answer, memories like importunate ghosts crowding in on him. "Annie Carson."

Moreland nodded, his expression very sombre. "Johanna Carson was a maid in our household for a period of about eighteen months. This was in the late 1970s."

"She obviously had a double," Daniel said his eyes flashing. "My mother was born in England. She came to Australia as a child with an aunt, her guardian. Her parents were killed in a motorway pile-up. That was the story anyway. Her aunt reared her but they split up when her aunt married someone my mother didn't like. My mother was on her own from a young age. She never travelled outside Queensland. She never travelled anywhere. She didn't have the money. She certainly didn't visit the Northern Territory. She is *not* this Johanna Carson. She *can't* be."

Moreland waited until Daniel finished his quiet tirade, before producing another photograph. "Look at this."

"I'm not sure I want to see it," Daniel said. "I'm sorry."

"Please, my boy," Moreland pleaded. "This was my reason for meeting."

"Very well then. I can't say…" Daniel froze in midsentence. Moreland's face had gone from handsome to haggard in a matter of moments. "Are you're all right, sir?" he asked in alarm. "Can I get you anything? You've lost all colour."

"Maybe a brandy," Moreland suggested.

Daniel didn't wait to signal a waiter; he fetched one. The waiter bolted away and reappeared with a brandy on a small silver tray in under twenty seconds.

Moreland took a slow draft then straightened his shoulders which as a young man would have been as wide as Daniel's. The blood rushed back into his face. "Ah, that's better. This isn't easy for either of us, Daniel, but we have to get through it."

To calm him, Daniel took the much newer looking photograph that Moreland had set down on the table.

He pored over it, recognising his own face, albeit the subject was a young woman. "Who *is* this?" he asked, casting a troubled glance at Moreland.

Moreland looked at him in the kindliest way possible. "It's my granddaughter, Cecile."

"She's very beautiful," Daniel remarked, not considering for a moment it followed he had to be very handsome. "How old is she?"

"Twenty-four." Moreland smiled, looking much better. "She's in Scotland at the moment and loving it. She's chief bridesmaid to a close friend who's marrying into Scottish aristocracy if you please. A whole week of festivities is planned."

"One can only wonder at how different her life has been to mine," Daniel said not without a certain bitterness.

Moreland leaned forward, his tone gentle. "I came to ask you Daniel if you would allow a blood test?"

Without giving himself time to think, Daniel shook his head vehemently. "I'm sorry, sir, no. What does it really matter now? My mother was a tragic figure. She's dead now. Personally I don't give a damn who my father was. Whoever he was he didn't want me."

"Have you considered, Daniel, he might not have known about you?" Moreland asked with a sad smile. "Your mother mightn't have been given the chance to tell him she was pregnant?"

"Whomever *he* was," Daniel answered with a harsh brittle laugh. "I don't think we should continue this conversation at the moment, sir. It's causing you great upset and it's certainly not helping me. In any event it doesn't change anything. We can't rewrite history."

"We can remake the future, Daniel," Moreland said with such a hopeful expression on his face Daniel turned his head away abruptly not wanting to be moved by it.

It was then he caught sight of Sandra, his dream and his desire but as far away from him as the moon. He felt the hot pulsing beat of his blood. She looked absolutely *beautiful* in a summery outfit he had never seen before. She must have just bought it he realized. She hadn't worn it on the plane, nor did he think she had it with her. She was walking buoyantly as a dancer does, threading her way through the tables, a lovely smile on her face.

It was difficult to take his eyes off her but Daniel turned back to Moreland speaking in an undertone. "This is Sandra now. She's looking forward to meeting you. Is someone waiting for you, sir, your chauffeur?'

Moreland laughed softly, correctly interpreting Daniel's look of concern and glad of it. "I've had a shock, Daniel as you have, but don't worry, I'm quite all right. In fact my doctor tells me I'll live to one hundred. Such are the ironies of life. My chauffeur is out the front, yes. We'll talk again when you've had more time to absorb what I've shown you. Meanwhile I want you to take those." He indicated the photographs on the table.

Not quite understanding why he did it, Daniel quickly thrust the photographs into his inner breast pocket, a little embarrassed by how vehement he had become about them.

Both men stood up as Sandra reached their table, looking lit from within. A lot of people in fact were caught up in watching her. Daniel introduced them, Moreland clearly enchanted, but as Sandra sat down for a few moments, she said in fascination, "Surely I've met you before, Mr. Moreland? Perhaps when I was a child?"

Moreland smiled back. "I couldn't possibly have forgotten *you*, Sandra."

"Then how do I explain it?" Her dark blue eyes were full of wonder. "There must be something in this other life business." She laughed.

Moreland stroked his chin. "Millions of people believe in it. Your observation interests me, Sandra. I know your uncle Lloyd of course and your cousin Bernard but I've always thought I should have met you, Trevor's daughter, Rigby's granddaughter. Perhaps you can visit me at my home some time soon. We should get to know one another. Who knows I may be of service? Daniel can bring you."

"Why, I'd love that, thank you." Sandra said, giving Daniel several quick questioning looks. Daniel was looking extremely sober, even upset, as though the meeting hadn't gone at all the way he wanted.

They sat talking pleasantries for ten minutes more. Eventually Daniel and Sandra accompanied Joel Moreland to his car, a stately Bentley. His

chauffeur who had been in casual conversation with
a hotel employee sprang to attention. "But you have
a dimple just like Daniel," Sandra remarked in some
wonder, turning to Joel Moreland as Daniel momen-
tarily moved off. "The *same* side of your face. You
have silver-grey eyes as well. One sees them rarely.
Is there some connection? Is that possible?" She
stared into those eyes. "There is, isn't there? I feel
it in my soul."

Moreland simply smiled. "Women never cease to
amaze me." He continued to hold Sandra's hand.

It wasn't just the eyes and the dimple, it was the
charm, Sandra thought, all sorts of thoughts whirling
through her head. A question was about to tumble
out only Daniel, who had been stopped by a passing
acquaintance, was about to rejoin them.

"Don't forget my invitation now," Moreland said,
relinquishing Sandra's hand.

"I definitely won't." Sandra was still rooted to
the spot. Just like Daniel, Moreland towered over her
in the same reassuring nonthreatening way. "Is this
our secret?" she asked, her mind racing with
powerful intimations.

"We have to work on it, Sandra," he told in a
sober voice.

CHAPTER NINE

DANIEL waited for the Bentley to pull away before he turned to Sandra to ask, "Have you had something to eat?"

"You're always trying to feed me, Daniel." She tried a laugh, a little daunted by the gravity of his expression. "I've been shopping actually." She looked down at her dress, hoping that he liked it. She'd bought it to gain his attention.

"You look like a ray of sunlight," he said, but unhappiness touched his eyes.

"You're upset about something, aren't you?" Sandra didn't care what he thought. She took his hand. She *was* his friend, wasn't she? Even if he wouldn't allow anything more. She was still working on it.

"Does it show?" He gave her a wry glance.

"And Joel Moreland has something to do with it? Why don't we have a coffee by the water?" she suggested. "It's a beautiful day. I'd forgotten Darwin Harbour is so immense. The deep turquoise of the water is amazing. You can fit in another coffee can't you?"

"Whatever you want." He made no attempt to let go of her hand. In fact to Sandra's tremulous joy he continued to hold it while they crossed the street and made their way to a harbour front coffee shop where one could sit outside beneath big blue and white umbrellas. Sandra ordered a cappuccino and a sandwich. Daniel settled for an espresso.

"Are you sure that's all you want?" he asked, sounding concerned coffee and a sandwich weren't substantial enough. She was still light enough for a zephyr of wind to blow her away.

"That's plenty," she said, anxious to get on with what was troubling him. "I want to hear all about your meeting. Please tell me."

"You *know,* don't you?" He leaned forward abruptly, slipping off her sunglasses so he could stare straight into her eyes.

"I don't know *exactly* what it's all about, Daniel," she said carefully, "but I can see a resemblance between you and Joel Moreland."

"Moreland?" Daniel asked in a voice that cracked in surprise. "Then you're seeing a lot more than I can."

Sandra's expression softened. "Whether you can see it or not, there *is.* Don't be distracted by age and the silver hair. I bet his hair was once as black as yours. He has the height, the shoulders, the manner, the charm. You both have a dimple in your cheek and extraordinary silver-grey eyes. They're fairly *rare*, Daniel." She broke off as their order arrived.

Thoroughly unnerved, Daniel took a quick gulp that burned his mouth. "He wants me to take a blood test. I imagine one that establishes DNA."

"Good grief!" Sandra, about to take a bite of her sandwich, put it down again. "This is serious."

"I'm not taking any DNA test, Sandra," he said with considerable firmness.

"Okay." She soothed him. "I don't blame you."

"I know *nothing* for sure," Daniel said, wanting to reach across and take her hand. She offered such comfort. Since Sandra had come into his life he realised he no longer felt he walked alone.

"Well what you *do* know don't keep it to yourself. He must believe you could be family?"

"Who cares!" Daniel said shortly, then made an effort to collect himself. "Once, to have had a family would have mattered a great deal. It doesn't anymore."

"You can't forgive the fact the man who fathered you abandoned your mother and his unborn child," Sandra observed, in an understanding voice.

"Would *you* forgive it?" Daniel threw down the challenge.

"No I would not." Sandra picked up a sandwich and bit furiously into it. "So if you and Joel Moreland are related as it does appear, your father would have been his son who was killed. Jared, wasn't it?"

Daniel's eyes flared as though he couldn't bear the answer. "Here, take a look at these." He withdrew the photographs Moreland had given him passing Sandra the one of his mother first.

Sandra held the photograph in her hand, studying it with intense interest. It was of a very pretty vulnerable looking young woman with haunting dark eyes. "This is?" She guessed it had to be his mother although Daniel bore the young woman no easily discernible resemblance.

"It's a photograph of a young woman who worked for the Morelands in the late 1970s," he said in a strained voice. "Her name was Johanna Carson. My mother was known as Annie Carson."

Sandra kept her eyes on the old photograph. "You're Annie Carson's son. You would *know* if this was your mother."

"I'm afraid it is." Daniel sighed deeply as though he didn't want to talk about it. "Everything she told me, I believed *all* of it. I think now, most of it was probably not true. My entire childhood and my whole adult life I've believed what little my mother told me."

"Believing one's mother is an article of faith, Daniel," Sandra pointed out gently. "My mother too dealt in fantasy."

"Maybe it's a problem with mothers," Daniel said. "Tell me what you make of this?" He passed her the second photograph.

Sandra found herself looking at a beautiful young

woman who could be Daniel's twin. "How extraordinary! Who is this?" She eyed Daniel cautiously.

"Moreland's granddaughter, Cecile."

Sandra acknowledged that piece of information in
silence. "Why produce these photographs *now?*" she
asked, tapping the photograph with her finger. "This
Cecile could be your twin. What's going on,
Daniel?"

Daniel's broad shoulders tensed. "How the hell
should *I* know."

"Why decide to acknowledge you *now?*" Sandra
frowned.

"Exactly."

Sandra fell into a thoughtful silence. "Do you
suppose if Jared Moreland were your father he
simply didn't know about you? Maybe he was killed
before your mother told him or he was killed before
they could do something about it. Maybe they
intended to get married?"

Daniel gave an off-key laugh. "My mother
worked as a domestic in their house. Moreland has
always been a rich powerful man. It's highly
unlikely he would have looked on such a union with
favour."

"I like him," Sandra said, her blue eyes burning
bright. "He seems the nicest, most trustworthy man.
I don't want to feel badly about him. I'm sure you
don't want to, either."

"No, I don't." Daniel admitted. "He said his sis-

ter-in-law only recently suggested the possibility
Jared had fathered a son."

"Did you believe he was telling the truth? You're
a good judge of men, Daniel."

"I was very taken with him," Daniel said. "I had this
strange feeling I *knew* him right from the minute we
shook hands. Both of us were upset. In fact he had a
bit of a sick turn which shook me up as well. All the
colour drained from his face. I had to get him a brandy.
I got the feeling he wants to make things *right*. Oh
God, I don't know, Sandra." Daniel looked away over
the glittering marina with its splendid yachts. "Even
if he is my grandfather I don't fit into his world. He
just can't walk into mine and think I'm going to do
anything he wants. I'm not stooping to any DNA test.
Not now, not ever! I'm someone else entirely from
that. I'm going to make my own way, thank you, not
become Joel Moreland's illegitimate grandson, for
God's sake. I'm *me!*" he said wrathfully.

"Could I dare put a word in here?" Sandra asked,
staring into his taut face.

"Best to stay out of it, Sandra."

"Sorry, Daniel. I'm *in* it, remember? Maybe Mr.
Moreland is trying to steal you away from me? It's
not on. You're *mine* until your year is up or you've
had enough of me."

His stormy expression lightened. "I couldn't ask
for a better boss," he said, hoping his smile was on
straight.

"You're the boss, Daniel," Sandra said, "but I'm learning."

"You haven't wasted a minute. You're really smart, Ms Kingston."

"Then can you let Mr. Moreland explain?" she urged. "He wants us to visit him some time soon."

He gave her one of his long glittery-eyed looks. "I'll take you any time you want, but the other has nothing to do with you, Sandra, so don't get in the middle of it. If Joel Moreland thinks he's going to recognise me now—subject to a DNA test of course—" he added caustically, "it's all too late."

Sandra put out a hand and grabbed his wrist. "Daniel, will you listen to me for a second?"

"No, I won't," he said in a dangerous voice. "You find it too easy to twist me around your little finger. Eat your sandwiches, Sandra. Your coffee must be cold. Mine is." He put up his hand to signal the waiter. "I'll order fresh."

The sun rose higher. The bush was quiet except for bursts of unrivalled merriment from the blue winged kookaburra perched on the sturdy limb of a red river gum. These majestic trees soared to one hundred and twenty feet and more forming a marvellous corridor of green along Jirra Jarra Creek. It was one of the favourite haunts of Sandra's childhood. Scarcely an inch of the great gums went unexploited much like the multistorey apartment towers in the city. Ravens, hawks, owls, magpies and even the great wedge-tailed eagles nested on the upper branches; brilliant parrots, laughing kookaburras, bigger birds and magpies underneath; bats, possums, reptiles in the hollows. Even the fallen branches and thick leaf debris protected ground nesting little birds, insects and tiny reptiles like the fierce little horny lizard. There were more lizards in Australia than anywhere else in the world, the most spectacular of them in her desert home.

Away from the brilliant glare of the plains the peace and cool of this green sanctuary was exquisite. The creek's deep dark green waters were said by the station aboriginals to possess healing powers not only for the health but behavioural problems as well. She and Berne along with the station children had swum here all the time with a stout rope tied to a high branch of a river gum allowing them to *fly* into the water or across the stream like Tarzan and Jane. Berne hadn't benefited much from the sacred waters. He appeared to be the same as he ever was, causing Sandra to believe he would be a whole lot better off starting a new life elsewhere. Her uncle was a lot easier to get on with these days, mollified no doubt by her genuine interest in his encyclopaedic knowledge of Austra-lian wildflowers. He was presently getting ready for another field trip to a remote pocket of Western Aus-tralia, a State renowned for the magnificence and sheer abundance of its native flora. A man who loved flowers and plants with a passion couldn't be all bad she reasoned. She was an adult now and thinking like one. Her father's fatal plane crash which her mother had claimed was *murder* had to have been an accident. Only Fate had been responsible.

A little wind blew up, skittering along the green corridor, loosening the olive green leaves and the petals of some dusky pink wildflowers that grew in cylindrical clumps in this oasis-like area. The aboriginal women made a paste of these succulents using it to protect and soften the skin of the face. Sandra knew for a fact the paste was wonderfully soothing on cuts and scrapes. There was so much that was really effective in bush medicine she thought. Arranged around her were the striking dark red sedimentary rocks and boulders that littered the ancient landscape. They formed such a contrast with the cabuchon waters of the creek, the lime-green of the aquatic plants and reeds that shadowed the creek's banks and the smouldering blue of the sky.

She had been sitting there daydreaming for some time now; carrying on a lengthy inner dialogue. There was so much that was problematic in her life. Daniel's life too was as mixed up as her own. Now he was confronted by revelations that had stunned and angered him. Daniel had carried a very bad image of the man who had fathered him. That wasn't going to go away in a hurry. She knew as well as anyone what it felt like to be *unwanted*.

A commotion on the high ridge—the unmistakable sound of a motorbike—made her turn her head. It was approaching at speed. The unwelcome din in such a peaceful place caused a flight of iridescent painted ducks about to land on the creek's surface, to skim it for a few feet before soaring steeply up again; up, up, over the tops of the red river gums seeking quieter waters. The kookaburra held its position, giving way to ribald protest, cackling away for all it was worth without deigning to move off its perch.

"Shut that bloody kookaburra up!" Chris Barrett, the jackeroo, yelled to her. He rode down the track, braking to a flamboyant stop a few feet away from her. Never mind the fact the wheels of the bike tore up scores of wildflowers releasing their faintly medicinal smell. "One of the boys told me this was the likely place you would be." He gave her his cheeky grin; a young man who thought he could always talk his way out of trouble.

"Did they now," Sandra said, watching him dismount. A real show-off was Chris. "So why aren't you working with the rest?"

He took a seat atop a red boulder. "Give me a break. I've been chasing a flamin' stallion all morning. A real stroppy devil."

"I take it he got away?"

"Yes, he did," Chris said ruefully, "but we got the mares and yearlings, even a few foals. It's a fantastic sight watching those wild horses run. I'm going to miss it. Mind if I come and join you for a few minutes?"

"Sure," Sandra nodded, pitching a few more pebbles into the deepest part of the creek. "But you're looking forward to going home, being with your family—surely?"

Chris laughed. "Well yes and no. I've had a great time here. Dan is a marvellous bloke. All the men look to him. No mean achievement when he's so young. These guys are really tough, but Dan has earned their respect. He often used to stand between us and old rubber guts—sorry—" he flushed "—your grandfather. Every other day I expected to be sent packing even though Mr. Kingston and my grandfather knew one another from school days. Dan stood up for us all. By the same token we've all got to pull our weight. Even lightweight old me though I reckon I'm a lot less stupid now. I'm not exactly looking forward to knuckling down in the staid old family firm. I've grown used to all this wonderful *space,* the excitement and adventure, the company of my mates." He stared into her face, hoping he was hiding his tremendous crush. "You're not going to sell the place, are you, Sandra?"

"Almost certainly not, since you ask." Sandra glanced back at the motorbike. "Daniel has been giving me lessons. I'm pretty good, if I say so myself."

"That's the word around the traps." Chris grinned.

"Want to show me?" His bright hazel eyes dared her.

"I might another time." Not that Daniel would actually *see* them, Sandra thought, sorely tempted. She loved the bike as a means of transport and she happened to know Daniel was working at the Five-Mile.

"What about I give *you* a spin?" Chris suggested eagerly. "You're game to get on with me, aren't you?" He pushed to the back of his mind Daniel had cautioned him never to take Ms Kingston on board as a pillion rider.

"I don't see why not." She responded to the cocky grin. "Ten minutes following the stream, then back again so I can collect the mare. Don't dare take off like a bat out of hell, either."

Chris rolled his eyes. "The last thing I would ever do is cause you fright. Daniel would kill me. Climb on. Just don't tell him about this. I couldn't predict what he'd do if we took a tumble."

It was Berne who drove into the Five-Mile holding camp, his handsome face wearing an expression that could be interpreted as I-told-you-so.

"That fool Barrett has come off the motorbike at the creek," he yelled to Daniel as though it was entirely *Daniel's* problem.

Daniel strode over to the four-wheel-drive. "Is he hurt?" Daniel was both irritated and concerned.

"He's broken his arm," Berne offered with little sympathy. "Sandra is with him. She's all shook up."

"What do you mean, Sandra's with him?" Daniel's face twisted into an expression of alarm. "She wasn't riding pillion, was she?"

"You know Sandra." Berne shrugged with a flicker of grim satisfaction. In their childhood Sandra had always been the favourite, Number One. "She's the same reckless little devil she ever was."

"She hasn't broken anything?" Daniel asked, his voice deepening in dismay.

"Settle down," Berne said, not unkindly. He hadn't wanted his cousin to actually *break* anything. "She's got a few scrapes and bruises but she's okay. She's worried about Barrett of all things and I suppose she got a bit of a fright."

"I'll come back with you," Daniel said, realizing afresh how jealous Berne was of his cousin. He moved swiftly to the passenger side. "I've *warned* Chris never to offer Sandra a ride."

"So I guess he's in contempt," Berne observed, wryly. He'd disliked that smart alec jackeroo from day one.

"You're mad at me," Sandra said as soon as she saw Daniel's taut expression.

"That's correct," he said in a clipped voice, going down on his haunches and feeling for her pulse. She was very pale but not clammy. "Do you feel giddy,

any nausea?" It was time for Chris to go back home.
He'd make sure of that.

Sandra couldn't fail to pick up the vibes. Anxiety
for Chris's job begin to gnaw at her. Not that Chris
didn't need his comeuppance given the reckless way
he had handled the powerful machine. Showing off,
of course, but they had taken quite a spill. "I'm fine,"
she said, when she was feeling anything but fine.

Daniel's eyes flashed like coins in the sunlight.
"Well you can thank your lucky stars for that," he
said crisply, turning his attention to the ashen face
Chris who was doing his best not to faint from the
pain. "How's it going?"

"Bloody awful," Chris murmured in a hollow
voice, aware of Daniel's contained anger.

"Why don't we shed a tear?" Berne chimed in sarcastically.

"Ah, shut up, Bernie." Sandra gave her cousin a
weary glance before addressing Daniel. "I've made
him as comfortable as I can."

"Good." Daniel had already noted with approval
she had padded Chris's lap with their hats and her
rolled up cotton shirt to support the injured limb.
Now she was left wearing a blue cotton singlet that
showed off her delicate breasts.

"It was the best I could do with what was at hand,"
she offered apologetically, thinking it a miracle she
had escaped more serious injury. Fortunately she
had been thrown off onto the sand whereas Chris's

body balanced the other way had fallen on heavier ground with the bike half on top of him.

"That's fine." Daniel spoke quietly though he felt a mad urge to let off steam. "We'll have to get you to hospital, Chris," he said. "What about the chest area, your ribs? Have you any difficulty breathing?"

"No," Chris gasped. "Look I'm sorry, Daniel."

"Forget that now." Daniel rose to his feet. "You'll need an X-ray to be sure there's no other damage." He looked at Berne. "Give me a hand to get him into the back seat, will you, Berne? We'll try to limit as much movement to your arm as we can, Chris, but be prepared for some pain."

"I deserve it," Chris mumbled, blinking several times to shake off the faintness. "I was pretty well showing off."

"I figured as much." Daniel nodded curtly before turning back to Sandra. "Sit there until I come back for you, Sandra," he said. "You've had a shock and there's a gash above your elbow."

"It's nothing," she said, twisting her arm around to look at something she scarcely felt. "Just bleeding a bit."

"Using up a fair bit of your luck, aren't you?" Berne asked her. "A bloke over on Gregory Downs was killed only the other day when he came off his bike. Broke his neck."

"Would you mind holding those stories for now, Berne," Daniel said, his sculpted features drawn taut.

"I doubt if she'd take any notice anyway," Berne said. "And Chris here is just a big-time show-off."

It was hard to argue with that.

Chris was airlifted to hospital where the fracture to his arm was confirmed.

"Why did you do it?" Daniel asked Sandra who was slumped tiredly into a planter's chair on the verandah. He picked up the cold beer Meg had brought him and downed it. It was a short while after sunset. The world was for a short time enveloped in a beautiful mauve mantle. The evening star was out. Soon it was joined by a million diamond pinpricks that quickly turned into blazing stars.

"Maybe I have a problem with authority figures?" Sandra suggested, very much on the defensive.

"You mean *me*."

"Yes, you, Daniel. I can see you're angry with me for breaking the rules."

"I'm angrier with Chris," he answered. "I told him not to take you on."

"Surely that's a lot to ask?" There was a slight quiver in her voice.

"No it isn't," Daniel said. "I'm in charge of the men, Sandra. I'm running this station for you until you're ready to run it yourself. Maintaining authority is important. I told Chris not to offer you a ride because I've learned a lot about him since he's been here. He's careless, he's cocky and I can't trust him. It's imperative to wear a helmet yet neither of you had one on. This is rough country, not a country lane. What if you'd sustained a head injury? What if *he* had? His mother was upset enough when I called her about his broken arm."

Sandra was mortified. "Okay we made a mistake, Daniel I'm sorry. We won't do it again."

"No, you won't," he said with emphasis. "When Chris is well enough he's going home. He's fired."

Sandra sat forward, aghast. "Who do you think you are?"

He drained his beer and set down the glass. "Sandra, I have to have my say out here unless *you* want to fire *me!*"

"Is that an ultimatum?" Her blue eyes started to blaze. She hated falling out with Daniel.

"It is," he said without hesitation. "It's for me to call the shots, Sandra. I'm responsible for the safety of the men and consider how many more times I feel responsible for *your* safety. I'm not objecting to your getting on the back of a motorbike *with* your helmet on. I'm objecting to your doing so with Chris Barrett who thinks he can do as he pleases because he's only fooling around for a time before he goes home to work for his rich old man. I'm not at all sympathetic to the way he acted even if I'm sorry he broke his arm. And you didn't answer my question?"

"What was it?" She sighed, resting back again.

How could she possibly fire Daniel. He was everything in the world to her.

"Are you going to let me run things as I see fit?" he asked.

"Next question?"

"How do you feel?" His voice changed and a different light came into his eyes.

"Like a bad, bad, girl. I don't like it when you're disappointed in me, Daniel."

"I don't like it when you give me a fright," he pointed out, remembering the force of his reactions. "The damned fool could have killed you and himself. Berne is quite right. There was a fatal accident on Gregory Downs. All the poor guy did was hit a pothole. His helmet wasn't on properly...it rolled off. Life on the land has its hazards, Sandra. I don't have to tell you that."

"As long as you still love me." She pulled a face at him. "And if you say you *don't,* you're fired!"

A look of amusement crossed his mouth. He allowed his eyes to rest on her as she lay back in the high backed peacock chair. One slender, silky fleshed arm was thrown lazily over the side, the injured arm he had cleaned and bandaged for her resting quietly in her lap. The glow from the exterior lamp mounted on the wall behind her, turned her hair to a glittering aureole. Her skin had the translucence of a South Sea peal. He could never tire of looking at her. *Never!*

"That's blackmail, wouldn't you say?" he asked, managing to sound casual.

"Whatever it takes, Daniel," she answered.

CHAPTER TEN

LLOYD KINGSTON had to seek his niece's permission to have either Daniel or Berne fly him to Perth, the capital of the adjoining vast State of Western Australia where he would be staying with a long-time friend, the well-known botanist, Professor Erik Steiner who was going to accompany him on his expedition. Daniel couldn't afford the time, so it was decided Berne would fly the Beech Baron into Perth.

"I wouldn't mind staying on for a week," Berne remarked to his cousin rather tentatively for him, "that's if you can spare the Baron. I know you can spare me. I've always liked Perth. I've got quite a few friends there."

"You'll have to check with Daniel, Berne," Sandra said in a calm, helpful way. "If it's okay with him it's okay with me. A week mind. We've got the helicopter but one never knows when the plane might be needed."

"True," Berne acknowledged. "Daniel's got to be

very important around here, hasn't he?" he added, almost sadly.

"Well he *is* running the place, Berne." Sandra was careful to answer reasonably. "*You* don't want the job."

"No way!" Berne threw up his hands as if to show that was way beyond his ambitions.

"What would you like to do?" Sandra asked, sounding like she really wanted to know and perhaps help him.

For once he saw her sincerity. "Something to do with aircraft," he said. "I'm a good pilot. Ask Daniel. Maybe not as good as him but good all the same. I love flying. I'd love to captain a jumbo jet flying all around the world."

"Can't you train for that?" she asked, surprised he wasn't already doing it if that was his ambition. "Heavens, you're young enough. You have the money to support yourself through your training. Seize the moment, Berne. Make enquiries in Perth. Jumbo jets aside, you could start your own charter business if you wanted to. Elsa could help you there. Surely she and her first husband were among the first to pioneer Outback charter flights?"

"Yeah." Berne thought for a minute. "She can fly, did you know? She's let her licence slip for years now but she can fly a plane. In fact she knows a hell of a lot about aircraft. She's very secretive, Elsa. She likes to act the dotty old lady. God knows why. I was trying to think the other day when it started. Dad reckons after Uncle Trevor was killed."

Sandra stared at him. "Of course I knew about the charter company, but she never flew the Cessna that I remember."

"Maybe not, but she could. There are a lot of things you don't know, cousin. Why would you? You were only a kid when you left. Your sweet mother did everything she could to paint Dad in the worst possible light. You can't imagine what it did to him, her claiming he sent his own brother to his death. If your mother could have had Dad convicted she would have. No wonder he hates her."

Sandra could see that would be the case. "I'm sorry about that, Berne," she said, all sorts of emotions swirling around inside her. "In many ways you, me, Uncle Lloyd and Elsa too have had a tough time. Elsa must have gone into marriage with Grandad thinking she was going to get something out of it. I don't mean material things, but whatever she craved, she didn't get it. Looking back I'm sure it wasn't *all* Grandad's fault. I've never acknowl- edged that before but I can see now it might have been true. What happened to Elsa is a mystery. But I want *you* to know if you'll let me I'll be your friend."

Berne had a sudden overpowering need to believe her. "You really want that? We never got on. I was jealous of course. You got all the attention."

"Didn't last long Berne," she sighed. "We were both deprived kids. Neither of us got enough love or attention. We suffered in our own way. But there's no need to be jealous of me any more. You can have your own life. A different life, one that suits you. Spend all your energies on becoming an airline pilot, as that's what you want. Shake on it, reconciliation?"

"Sure." Berne gripped her outstretched hand, drawing a deep, shaky breath. "I guess it is better to have you onside, Sandra."

"You bet it is." Sandra smiled.

They were on their own! Sandra couldn't believe her good fortune. Elsa and Meg were in the house of course, but essentially they were on their own. It was a *sumptuous* feeling and she was determined to take full advantage of it. During the day she joined Daniel as often as she wanted. The evenings were spent over a leisurely dinner, a short walk around the grounds afterwards, then they retired to the study where the intensive but stimulating learning sessions continued. There was so much to learn about the business and Sandra was anxious to make her contribution.

Midweek something strange happened. Sandra awoke with the unnerving feeling *someone* was in or had just left her room. Not only that there was a faint rattling noise. She sat up quickly in the bed, her eyes trying to pierce the gloom. There was no moon to send its illuminating rays across the verandah and into her room. She desperately needed light.

"Who's there?" The words were on her lips before she even got to flick a switch.

She stared around the room, her body trembling though she wasn't cold. Not the slightest sign of disorder. She was a naturally tidy person. Everything was in its place. Just a bad moment she thought. Some lingering dream. She'd had a full day joining in on a muster for clean skins the men knew they had missed in dense scrub. She'd enjoyed the experience but in the end the heat and the physical exertion had gotten to her. Before bed she'd been forced to take a couple of painkillers for her headache. Elsa had rustled them up from her stockpile.

Her accelerated heartbeats were slowing. She breathed deeply, punching her pillows a few times to get them into the right shape. A glance at her bedside clock told her it was 3:00 a.m., the witching hour. The temptation to get out of bed and go across the hallway to Daniel was so acute she groaned with the pain of it. She could tip toe across his room, rest her hand upon his sleeping shoulder.

"Daniel, it's *me!*"

He'd awaken; recognise the scent of her, draw her wonderingly down onto the bed. He would gather her into him, his body against hers, telling her he wanted her urgently. His beautiful mouth would unerringly find hers. She would open it to him… His hand was on her breast. She's holding on to him, clutching him. One of her arms is locked around him, the other is buried in the raven thickness of his hair. Delicious shudders are passing through her. She's guiding his hand, wanting his fingers to slip inside her. God, she's been thinking about it all the time, wicked girl!

Only it wouldn't happen like that at all. She sobered abruptly, ashamed of the illicit pleasure she was taking. Daniel would bundle her up and escort her back to her room. No seduction scenes for Daniel. If it were ever going to happen he wouldn't let it happen in her own house. Daniel had *huge* problems with making love to her. She knew that. It was almost as if he were up against a serious taboo or he was heeding lots of signs tacked up everywhere saying, Keep Off. It is just stupid, she thought, when we both want it. She wasn't such a fool she didn't know how he watched her.

Better check the door.

She knew perfectly well it was locked. She had gotten into the habit of locking it even with Daniel in the house. If it looked like she didn't trust her family, she didn't care though these days her anxieties seemed absurd. Her mother's perspective had been warped. She slipped out of bed and padded across the room, listening for noises in the house.

Not that she would hear them. The old homestead had been built of stout timbers, mahogany and cedar.

She was halfway across the spacious room when she paused, staring at the floor. There was something on the rug. Little beads. Sandra crouched down to pick them up. The beads were scattered, six in all. Jade beads. The fact someone really had been in her room hit her like a punch in the stomach. She turned on the chandelier flooding the bedroom with light. She found one more bead closer to the door. They had poured off a necklace. Sandra reached for the brass doorknob. The door was still locked. So how then had someone come to stand in the deep shadows watching her?

She started to think of an intruder coming by way of the verandah. There was a white lattice door at the end of the wing, usually locked. The other day she'd found a tiny scrap of fabric impaled on it but hadn't thought much of it. It could have come off one of Meg's dresses or even one of the house girls' Meg was training.

When a dingo's mournful howl carried on the desert air her nerve broke. Sandra unlocked her door and fled across the hallway to Daniel's room, assuming it too would be locked but it wasn't. She burst in. She couldn't help it, not doing anything appalling like screaming but rushing towards the bed, calling his name.

"Daniel, Daniel, wake up!"

Something *huge* was in her way. Hell, a damned chair! She swore fiercely, holding a hand to her throbbing shin. "Daniel!"

"Sandra, what the hell!" Daniel sprang to his feet, straight as a lance. He had thought that voice belonged in his dream. But no, she was *there,* in his bedroom swearing her head off.

"Where's the light?" she was yelling. "I don't want to run into another great hulking chair. What's it doing in the middle of the room anyway?"

Immediately he switched on the bedside lamp seeing her standing in the centre of his room *irradiated.* She was wearing the flimsiest little nightdress he could ever imagine. No concealing robe. Not even slippers on her feet. She was clutching something in her hand.

"Sandra, what are you doing here?" he asked, all his senses instantly raised to the nth power. "Do you know what time it is?"

"What's time got to do with it, Daniel?" She looked at him with highly critical blue eyes. Not that there was anything to criticise. He could have posed for a Calvin Klein ad for boxer shorts for that's all he was wearing. Brief navy boxer shorts with a white stripe down the side..

"It's the only few hours I get to sleep," he explained.

"When you promised me you'd be on call." She moved to close the distance between them and he sprang back.

"What's the *matter* with you?" She eyed him

sternly. "Anyone would think I was going to give you an electric shock."

"Allow me to put some clothes on would you, Sandra?" he asked tightly, circling a finger so she would turn away.

"If you must." She gritted her small teeth.

"I must." Swiftly he pulled on a pair of jeans and zipped them up. "I don't mean to criticise your behaviour in any way—you are after all my boss—but is there something you want?" They faced one another again, Daniel's dark polished skin gleaming in the light.

He had a light V shaped mat of dark hair on his chest that disappeared into his low slung jeans.

"Well it's not *sex* if that's what's worrying you," she snapped. "I mean would I do anything so crass as to jeopardize our friendship?" she added caustically. "No, the thing is, Daniel, someone was in my room just now."

"You're kidding!" He was in something of a daze. This *was* happening, wasn't it? She was in his bedroom in a sheer little nightie with her tousled cap of buttery curls and her eyes blazing like sapphires.

"I found these beads on the floor. Look."

Now she moved right up to his shoulder. His heart leapt. She might be pocket sized but she packed such a powerful sensual punch unless he was very strong she could defeat him easily. "Show me." Daniel forced his breath to stay even. "Jade, aren't they? Or nephrite." He stared down at the small polished olive-green beads. "Maoris use it as a talisman of protection. The Chinese believe it blesses all who touch it."

"I'm not trying to *sell* them to you, Daniel," she said testily.

Such a tart tongued glowing creature! "Let's take a look in your room then," he suggested. "You might like to put something on."

"Anyone would think you had to fight off my advances," she started muttering as she stalked into her bedroom, making a beeline for her yellow Thai silk robe. "There, feel safer now?" she asked tartly, tying the sash with exaggerated movements.

"You aren't the sweetest girl in the world, are you?" He looked around, frowning in concentration. "Where were the beads?"

"On the floor, just about here." She moved to the spot rubbing the pile of the Perisan rug back and forth with her bare toes. "I woke with the panicky feeling someone was in the room or just leaving it. I thought I heard a rattling sound. I knew my door was locked. I must have been dreaming. It wasn't until I decided to double-check the door when I saw them. They certainly weren't there when I put out the light. Someone was in the room, Daniel."

"You don't think you could have missed them earlier? They blend in with the rug strangely enough."

"Then how did I miss not *walking* over them?"

she asked as if she'd produced the trump card. "One was actually near the door."

"And it was locked?"

"*Yes,* Daniel."

"The only people in the house are you, me, Elsa and Meg. I can't think the house girls would meddle. You'll have to leave *me* out of it."

"Because of your vow?" She stared at him with huge challenging eyes.

"What vow?"

"The one you made as soon as we met. *Never lay a finger on her!*"

"So you know about that, do you?" he asked dryly.

"There's no logic to it, Daniel."

"Really? I consider to break it would be more like men acting badly. Now, shall we get back to the problem at hand? Your nocturnal visitor could only be Elsa or Meg or the resident ghost. I can't see Meg or Elsa paying you a call unless one of them sleep walks. Come to think of it, it does happen."

"Yes, like once in a blue moon," Sandra scoffed. "I didn't imagine any of this, Daniel."

"Hang on." He hesitated for a second looking down at her, then strode out onto the verandah.

She raced after him. "I found a scrap of material pinned to the lattice a few days ago," she told him breathlessly. The door was unbolted. She watched him as he shot the bolt home.

"It could easily have come off Meg's dress. Go back to bed, Sandra. I'll leave my door open and a light in the hall. No one is going to bother you."

"Well I *am* bothered," she said huffily.

"We'll leave it until morning to ask questions." They were back in her room, staring at one another. "Meg would never do anything to cause you concern. Elsa genuinely cares for you. You're sweet to her."

"I feel sorry for her, that's why. But she's just the type to do spooky things," Sandra felt a sudden chill. "No mouse could be quieter, though I can't think she'd wish to harm me. Can I ask you a question?"

"Fire away." He gave a single abrupt nod of his head.

"Do you wear jade beads?"

He didn't deign to answer.

"Just a thought. Would you like to stay with me, Daniel?" For some reason she had the wicked impulse to taunt him. "It's an awfully big bed. Our bodies wouldn't have to connect at all."

"Impossible, Sandra."

"I know, I'm ranting. I'm sorry." She stripped off her silk robe and threw it around one of the bedposts.

"You're not at all self-conscious of your body, are you?" he said, desire for her lashing at him like stockwhips.

"Well I'm not exactly a glamour model," she answered tartly. "What's to *see?*"

"Are you completely mad?" he rasped, astonished she could say such a thing.

Sandra spun around, furiously hurt. She rushed him very fast, hitting him in the chest. "How *dare* you say something like that to me, Daniel!"

To Daniel it was the straw that broke the camel's back. "That *does* it!" he ground out. He got an arm around her lifting her half off the ground and pitching her onto the bed with such strength she bounced.

"Daniel!" She sat up in astonishment and gulped.

"You have to stop playing games with me." He was breathing hard through flared nostrils, his powerful body tense, a vertical frown between his black brows, luminous eyes stormy.

"I will. I will," she promised. Fear didn't come into it. She wanted to *calm* him. "I'm sorry, Daniel. I wasn't trying to turn you on. Not *then* anyway." She couldn't lie to him.

"Well you did!" He knew it was wrong, but he was too tanked up with desire to be able to turn off the engine.

"Come here!" He swooped on her, dragging her up against him feeling her fingers sink into the mat of hair on his bare chest.

"*Daniel!*" She made a soft yielding sound, pressing herself against him.

For an instant he was worried his beard might rasp her lovely skin. "Little *witch!*" he said hotly.

"You should be using those little fists on me not urging me on." He clamped her small slender body still closer against him, revelling in her female softness and the alluring scents of her hair and skin. He wanted to know the *whole* of her...so badly...so badly. With a shudder he speared his fingers into those buttery curls pulling back her head so he could take her mouth. It seemed like an eternity since he had last kissed her. He had never stopped thinking about it, how beautiful it was. He had her *now!*

His mouth covered hers, not hard but voluptuously. He found the touch and the taste exquisite, to be savoured. A primitive adrenaline was pumping through his blood, assisting his sense of mastery. His hands had a life of their own. They strayed over her throat and delicate shoulders, moving towards those small tantalizing breasts. The V neckline of her nightgown had fallen low; low enough for him to fondle her naked flesh. Her nipples came erect under his urgent fingers while a little moan came from the back of her throat. She arched her back making it easier for him to take first one then the other into his mouth. He lifted his head. Watched her face. Her eyes were closed but the lids were flickering with sensation.

He pulled her in tight, wanting her wild and wilful on the bed. She had a little wildness in her. He *knew* it. He wanted to strip that lighter than air nightdress from her. He wanted her to feel his hands all over her, exploring that sweet tender body that gave off a million sparks when touched.

She was making sounds, little kittenish *mews* he found incredibly erotic. There was a heat inside him he had never experienced before. Did she know those little mews were pushing him further along the hot narrow path of temptation? By now his need for her was so fierce he couldn't be pushed *one* inch further. Every nerve in his body was *electric* for her. There was nothing he didn't want to do to her. All was permissible between lovers.

Wasn't that what he wanted to be, her lover? Her *only* lover.

"Daniel!" Bright little explosions like stars were going off in her head. She was literally swooning in his arms.

Daniel misread her ecstasy. To him it sounded like the fevered gasp of the tortured.

He recoiled sharply. What the hell was he doing? Ravishing a virgin? Ravishing this slip of a girl he had sworn to protect? That jolted his heart.

He released her so abruptly, she pitched forward, her head whirling while she tumbled to the floor. "Sandra!" He was stunned; sick with shame. He picked her up bodily, embracing her, before he laid her on the bed. "I hate myself if that's any comfort to you."

"It isn't!" Her voice was shaken, the sound vibrating inside her head. "You're a caveman."

"I don't doubt it. But you've made me. You're an enchantress."

"Daniel, do you *mean* that?" Suddenly she was full of hope. If she could enchant him she was really on to something.

"Listen, I'm going." Daniel read the swift speculation in her huge blue eyes. "I wanted to *ravish* you. I stopped just in time. Don't you realise that?"

How to convince him she was ready? "Wherever you want to take me, Daniel, I'm prepared to go," she said, mind and body flooded with love for him. "I never thought I was going to fall in love. I didn't even think I would *want* a man too near me. I thought the way my creep of a stepfather behaved towards me I was somehow damaged. I hated being the object of *lust*."

"Did you now!" Daniel was breathing fast, thinking if he stayed any longer he would really unravel. Her loveliness, her desirability was overwhelming. How was he supposed to combat all that? "I have to tell you, Sandra," he gritted, "*I* lust after you, too. There's a warning in there somewhere but you don't want to hear it."

"Then get out of my room if that's how it is!" She felt bitterly rejected.

"Don't worry, I'm going." He speared his fingers through his thick pelt of hair, dragging it back from his tense face. "It's damn near daybreak anyway. I'll leave my door open. I won't leave the homestead in the morning either until we find out exactly what went on here. Okay?"

"Morning can't come soon enough," she cried and punched the pillow.

CHAPTER ELEVEN

SANDRA slept so heavily she might have been drugged. In the morning Meg had to wake her to say they couldn't find Elsa. She wasn't in the house, nor anywhere in the home compound. Daniel had already sent out a search party to scour her usual haunts.

"She's getting on you know." Meg pleaded and re-pleated the edge of her white apron in her agitation. "Never sees a doctor and she should. She's often short of breath. Occasionally she wanders in her mind. You must have noticed that."

"Of course I have, Meg." Sandra was out of bed, fishing out clothes to put on. "She likes to visit the family cemetery. I hope Daniel will try there."

"I don't know about *likes*." Meg looked dubious. "More like she's *driven*. She does go there a lot. I'll let you get dressed, love. I've got a bad feeling about this."

It was when Sandra was halfway out the door she spotted out of the corner of her eye, a dark grey envelope that lay on top of the highboy.

"Wait a minute," she said aloud, though no one was listening. She retraced her steps reaching for the envelope. It was addressed to her.

"Oh, God!" Sandra knew at once it was from Elsa though she wasn't familiar with Elsa's handwriting. A sudden wave of nausea rolled through her, which was odd. She took up a position on the nearest chair opening the envelope and withdrawing its contents; two handwritten sheets of a lighter grey paper embossed with Elsa's initials EGK. Sandra found herself slumping back against the chair overtaken by a peculiar feeling of weakness and fatigue. She knew now from the bitter taste in her mouth and the unfamiliar sluggish feeling Elsa had given her not painkillers but some kind of sedative, maybe sleeping pills. It had been Elsa in her room, Elsa's broken beads. Elsa gliding around the house like a ghost.

What she read in stunned horror and disbelief was Elsa's *confession*. Her last words to anybody.

Alexandra, my dear, I find I can no longer continue. I know you will hate me now you learn the truth. I deserve your hatred. It was I who was responsible for your father's death no matter Trevor was the last person in the world I intended to harm. Trevor was always kind to me as you are. It was your grandfather, my husband, I wanted to see punished for the uncaring way he treated me. I wanted love. I got rejection. The pain and the humiliation became too much. He never loved me. I wasn't his beloved Catherine. I wasn't what he wanted at all. My first husband had all but destroyed me; your grandfather did the rest. It was Rigby who was to visit the outstation that day. Rigby sent Trevor at the very last minute. I had known what to do to the Cessna to cause it to crash. I did it without a qualm. Not much of a motive I know, but I was different then. Afterwards I was changed forever. The guilt stripped me of my sanity. I've suffered terribly for my crime, Alexandra. But there must be an end. Scatter my ashes far away from Moondai. Far away from your grandfather. I never belonged here. The sea might be the place. I never meant your father harm. I've visited his grave countless times begging his forgiveness. But my crime is unforgivable. I'll be made to suffer for it in the next life I'm sure. There's no escape.

Elsa.

Lloyd and Trevor returned to Moondai the very next day, the family closing ranks on the sudden death of a senior member. The cause of death was given as myocardial infarction or more commonly heart attack. It was noted, had Mrs. Kingston received emergency medical assistance or been close to a hospital she might have survived but she had chosen to take a long walk that day without telling anyone where she was heading. That alone had greatly lessened her chances of survival. It seemed Elsa had ignored many of the symptoms of heart disease for some considerable time without seeking help.

Whether Elsa had helped her death along, given her stated intention, Sandra would never know, but she couldn't withhold Elsa's secret from the family. They had a right to know.

"Poor Elsa," Lloyd said afterwards, without any sympathy at all. "She started going to pieces from that day on. As well she should. Her problems were all of her own making." He looked in a kindly fashion on his distressed niece. "My father did his best but pandering to a neurotic woman wasn't in his nature. It was the first husband leaving her that really destroyed Elsa. At least *I'm* in the clear," he added ironically.

"Tell me you forgive me," Sandra begged.

"Nothing to forgive." He patted her shoulder. "You were a child. You believed what you were told. Forgiving your mother is another matter. Are you going to tell her?"

Sandra shook her head. "I can't see any point in making this public, either. Elsa had her secret. I think as a family we have to keep it, otherwise we start up another pointless scandal. Elsa is dead. It's all over. Shall we take a vote on it?"

"Does Daniel know?" Berne asked.

"We've nothing to fear from Daniel," Sandra said.

"All the same…"

"Leave Daniel to me, Berne," Sandra said.

"Well that's it, I guess," Lloyd Kingston said. "To the world we've lost a dear family member. We're all sad which of course I'm not."

"So much of life is sad," Sandra said, thinking she would never get over the shock of it. "Elsa wanted her ashes to be scattered at sea."

"I'll take care of that," Lloyd offered. "She was my stepmother though she never took the time to be one. In many ways she was quite simply, *mad*. I'm going back to Perth as soon as I can. Berne can come with me. The trip will do him good. I understand he wants to be an airline pilot."

"Sure do." Berne smiled across at Sandra.

"Then good luck, my boy. You'd better get on with it. You'll have a lot to learn."

"No problem!" Berne appeared entirely comfortable with the idea.

There was a memorial service for the late Mrs. Elsa Kingston in Darwin. Dying so soon after her husband, people acquainted with the family shook their heads in sympathy prepared in death to overlook the fact the marriage had been a disaster.

Outside the church people pushed forward to introduce themselves, or reintroduce themselves, offering a word of condolence or respect. From time to time Daniel touched Sandra's elbow, dipping his dark head to murmur the names of people she didn't know. The healing process with her own family had started, but Daniel was the one person Sandra wanted beside her.

"It's Joel Moreland coming this way," Daniel alerted her, easily spotting Moreland's distinguished silver head among the crowd. "He has a lady with him. Seventies, beautifully dressed. The sister-in-law I'd say."

They approached, a handsome couple. Moreland looked even more impressive in his dark clothes. He certainly was a splendid looking man Sandra thought as introductions were made and respects paid. The lady *was* Moreland's sister-in-law, Helen, widow of a younger brother who had never enjoyed good health and died prematurely at fifty-six.

Helen Moreland tried, but couldn't conceal her shock at meeting Daniel, indeed her expression crumpled into tears.

"Now, Helen," Moreland took her hand in a comforting grasp. "It's all right, my dear."

"I just can't believe it that's all," Helen Moreland said, staring into Daniel's eyes. "He looks *exactly* like you at that age, Joel."

"I'm not sure I want to speak about this, Mrs. Moreland," Daniel said, very quietly.

She put her hand on his arm. "But you must, my dear. Not here, I know. But you *must* hear what I have to tell you."

"Perhaps you could join us at home," Moreland suggested. He looked from Daniel to Sandra, his eyes resting on her as though she were a powerful ally.

"I'm sorry, sir," Daniel said, courteous but firm.

Sandra turned to him immediately. "Perhaps you should, Daniel," she urged. Secrets turned into terrible burdens. The best thing Daniel could do was let Mrs. Moreland tell him what she knew.

"*Please,* Daniel." Helen Moreland lifted her gentle eyes that nevertheless missed nothing to his face. "Did you know Joel was christened Daniel Joel Moreland? His father was Daniel too so somewhere along the way to avoid confusion Daniel got to be Joel. Jared was christened Jared Joel Moreland."

"Where is this leading, Mrs. Moreland?" Daniel asked, intensity in his voice.

"Why don't we follow a bit later on?" Sandra smoothly intervened. "Any taxi driver will know where you live."

"If that's your wish." Joel Moreland inclined his silver head. "Or I could send my man back for you."

"I don't seem to have much choice, do I?" Daniel turned away from an intense scrutiny of Sandra to ask in an ironic voice.

"It's all *for* you, Daniel," Helen Moreland said.

"Perhaps an hour, Mr. Moreland," Sandra said quickly, linking an arm through Daniel's and holding on.

Moreland, the man with the Midas touch, nodded,

seemingly content to let a twenty-year-old girl handle things. "As you wish, my dear."

The fact they had reached a decision gave Sandra a new sense of purpose. Resistance, however, was coming off Daniel in waves. She knew and sympathized with the intensity of conflict going on inside him but she trusted her feminine intuition. The crowd had dispersed and the two of them had wandered off finding the same coffee shop they had visited once before.

"You don't want to go, do you?"

Daniel had removed his dark jacket in the heat. The dazzling white of his shirt made a striking contrast with his tanned skin. "You know damn well I don't," he replied, tersely, thinking he had done nothing but drink coffee over the last few days. "Though I've taken great note of the fact you seem determined to get me there."

"Maybe it's where you *belong*, Daniel," she said. "Ever thought of that?"

He dismissed that with a cursory wave of his hand. "I don't exactly belong anywhere. Most certainly not with the man with the Midas touch."

"Even though he could be your grandfather?" she asked, covering his hand with her own.

"Why are you doing this, Sandra?" He stared into her beautiful eyes, his own filled with emotion.

"Because I love you, that's why," she said briskly.

"Sandra." He bent his dark head over his hands

without looking up. She couldn't keep telling him she loved him otherwise he could never go away.

"No need to be embarrassed," she said cheerfully. "You know me. I rush in where angels fear to tread. You don't have to love me, okay? I can see you're obsessed with standing alone, but you need a little bit of a hand with this. I'm the right woman for the job."

He lifted his head again, finding those electric-blue eyes. "And a *little* hand is what you've got." He raised it to his lips and kissed it.

"People are looking, Daniel," she pointed out, love for him invading every part of her body.

"Fine. Who cares?"

"I thought you did?"

His eyes glittered. "How many people do you think know you're the rich Alexandra Kingston, mistress of historic Moondai station?"

"You want to pretend I'm not?"

"I wish with all my heart you weren't," he said, with intense feeling.

"Then I wouldn't be *me,* Daniel, would I? I know you care about me."

"I wouldn't be heading for the Moreland mansion if I didn't," he told her a shade harshly. He was lashing out in frustration when he loved her. Hell he knew it, but it was impossible to say. What could he offer her? Maybe in a year or two when he had time to get going. Hope reared its head. She looked so beautiful, so exclusive. She was wearing a little black suit with gold button detailing, a white silk blouse beneath the jacket, sheerest black stockings—he had never seen her in stockings—with a pair of high heeled black shoes on her feet. The shoes matched her handbag. No hat. Just her radiant curls that were growing longer and thicker by the day. He knew the outfit had been air freighted in. She'd told him she had nothing she could wear to a funeral in her wardrobe. Well she wore this outfit with considerable chic. She looked what she was: a lovely, fashionable heiress and thus way out of his league.

The meeting with the Morelands passed with far less difficulty than Daniel had anticipated. Helen Moreland who recognised Daniel was there to please Sandra more than anyone else, lost little time telling her story while Joel Moreland and Daniel, sat forward in their respective armchairs, their heads bent at *exactly* the same angle.

"I want to tell you the truth, Daniel," Helen Moreland began, "you know, the truth, the whole truth, nothing but the truth as I know it. The story is as old as time. A secret arrangement between two women. One powerful, one of lower station. The young scion of the family falls in love with a pretty young woman employed as a servant in the house. It was Jared's mother, Frances, who became aware of this attraction and found it utterly *unthinkable*.

She sent the girl packing while her husband was away on business and her son was enjoying what should have been a fun week with his friends which took in the Alice Springs annual rodeo. What tragic event happened next pushed all thought of a dismissed servant out of a wildly grieving mother's mind. For almost four years Frances was literally off her head with grief. She adjusted to the harsh reality of life in time but had never fully recovered. Frances adored her only son. She had such plans for him. She genuinely believed no blame could be attached to her for getting rid of a girl she considered little more than an opportunist. It wasn't until Frances lay dying that she told me she had a feeling—just a *feeling*— the girl could have been pregnant. She said she did try to trace the girl—this was some five years after Jared's death—but Johanna Carson had simply vanished with the money Frances had given her to disappear. But that *feeling*, remained. It must have haunted her, particularly as she kept it all to herself. After Frances died it took me quite a while to work up the courage to tell Joel. He'd had enough to bear but what if there was some truth in this feeling Frances had? Joel set an investigator to find out. The rest you know."

Joel Moreland looked up as his sister-in-law's voice faltered. "We have ample reason to believe you're Jared's son, Daniel," he said. "The son he never knew about because you were in your mother's womb. Knowing my son the way I did he would have stood by Johanna no matter what. As Helen said, my wife had great plans for Jared—she worshipped him almost to the exclusion of our lovely daughter—she already had a girl picked out for him. She would have been determined not to allow Johanna, your mother, to ruin those plans. God knows what would have happened only Jared was killed. It was all too late. And it *would* have been only Frances couldn't keep her secret to the end. She knew not to tell me. I would have been shocked out of my mind. We're talking my grandchild here! She chose to tell Helen."

"I tried to get her to tell you Joel," Helen said, emotional tears springing into her eyes. "But she was adamant you should never know. You would never have acted as Frances did. I believe Frances had *more* than a feeling Johanna was pregnant but she was already condemned as not being good enough for her son."

"A *nice, compassionate* woman," Daniel observed grimly.

"Your grandmother, Daniel," Joel Moreland reminded him, sadly. "I know how you feel, son. I understand perfectly. Perhaps if Jared had lived Johanna would have found the courage to tell him she was pregnant. Had I been at home more often; been more aware of what was happening in my own household I wouldn't have permitted my wife to sack her. I don't remember Johanna all that well, I'm sorry. I was so busy all the time, travelling around the country and overseas. Nothing worked for your mother, I'm afraid. Nor for you because of it. My wife's punishment was not only the loss of her son but her only grandson. That's *you*, Daniel. I know I asked you to allow a DNA sample but I didn't really want to anyway. I *know* you're my grandson."

"So do I," Helen Moreland added with untrammelled joy. "You're the image of Joel at the same age. You also have a look of Jared, though you have Joel's eyes. Cecile has them too. No one seeing you and Cecile together would doubt you were family."

"So what *is* it you expect me to do, sir?" Daniel addressed Joel Moreland directly.

A look of agonised longing passed over Moreland's distinguished face. "I want you to take your rightful place as my grandson, Daniel. Be in *no* doubt I would never have let Johanna go, knowing she was carrying my grandson. Your father would never have permitted it either. If you doubt it, you don't know me," he said emphatically.

Daniel believed him without hesitation. "How many people know about this?" he asked.

"For *sure*, only the four of us. Sandra—" Moreland turned his head to smile at her "—recognised the resemblance right off but then I sense she's very close to you?"

"Aren't you forgetting something, sir?" Daniel

asked bleakly. "Sandra is the Kingston heiress. I *work* for her."

Joel Moreland nodded. "I understand your feelings, Daniel. Your sense of pride and decency, but *you're* the Moreland heir. Don't you *want* to be?"

The question saw Daniel on his feet, obviously upset. "I'm sorry, sir. It's too much to handle." He shook his head.

"I understand that as well." Moreland rose to his full height, laying his hand on Daniel's shoulder. "You need time, Daniel. Time is on your side. Unfortunately it's not on mine."

"You're not ill?" Daniel asked with a rush of dismay.

"No, no," Moreland reassured him swiftly, "but I'm not young anymore. I'm not even middle-aged even if I don't feel so old. I'm a septuagenarian, Daniel."

"Like me." Helen Moreland smiled at them both, wondering how *anyone* could fail to see the resemblance. "I couldn't be more thrilled to meet you, Daniel. It's like a dream come true. Thank you so much for bringing him to us, Sandra." She reached out to take Sandra's hand. "Now that we've met, you can't go away, either."

A lot more than the words said was communicated through the women's eyes.

Just as Sandra guessed, Daniel, with a fixed determined look in his eyes insisted on moving back into the overseer's bungalow.

"We're in the middle of nowhere, Sandra," he told her as they rode out to the holding yards. A road train was due in around noon to transport a mob of prime cattle to market. "There's not a single soul on the station who would harm a hair of your head. Your uncle and cousin have left for Perth. They were never any threat even if they've been damned unpleasant up until very recently. It was all in your mother's mind, sad to say although she was right about one thing. The crash was no accident. Meg is in the house and I'm near enough for you to yell if you want me. I'd be with you in a trice. I can't stay in the house, you can see that?"

"Certainly," she answered mockingly, watching a small group of nomadic emus feeding on some dry seeds in the ground. Emu oil had been used for countless centuries by the aboriginals for a variety of ailments. These days it was having great success easing the pain of arthritis. She had to think about that one. Lord knows there were enough emus running wild on Moondai. "You're scared I'll barge into your room." She turned her head back to Daniel. He looked marvellous in the saddle, all lithe athleticism, a superb horseman.

"You bet I am," he said. "I'm scared what I might do."

"Could I believe…consider having sex?"

"It's okay for you, to joke. By the time you got around to yelling *stop,* you'd have pushed me right over the edge."

"There's a cure for being a virgin, you know. I think that's what's worrying you."

"You want to stop teasing, Sandra," he warned. "In my book there are certain rules of behaviour."

"Does this mean you're going to keep me at arm's length until we're married?"

"You can stop that right now," he admonished, noting the cheeky mocking look on her face. "Besides, did I ever mention I love you?"

"If you had any brains you would," she answered, smartly. "Sandra, I love you more than life itself!" She assumed a melodramatic voice, quickly reverting to her normal tones. "*That* would be nice. And that's not *all*, as any good salesman would say. There's an added incentive. The house comes with me. There's tons of room for future kids. Try to see it my way, Daniel. There's only one word for us. It's *soul mates!*"

He gave a short laugh. "Then this soul mate has a lot of soul searching to do."

"I know," she sighed, riding her mare in closer. "Daniel there's nothing wrong with admitting to being Joel Moreland's grandson. He's a lovely man. A lovely, *lonely* man. You could think of him."

"I expected you to say something like that, Sandra. Thing is, I'm thinking of my mother."

"I am too, Daniel," she said with utter sincerity. "I could never be insensitive to what your mother went through. But had she lived long enough I don't think she would have told you to deny this relationship. In a way it's a vindication of all the sacrifices that went before. Frances Moreland paid for what she did. I just don't think you and your grandfather should have to suffer her mistakes any longer. It's not as though I'm doing myself any good, saying this. You become a Moreland, where does that leave me? I'm sending you off to join the competition when I desperately *need* you."

"I'll be here as long as you need me, Sandra," he promised, a flash coming into his eyes. "When I get my life straightened out we can talk."

Well at least we've got *that* cleared up, Sandra thought. She knew she only had to sit still and she'd get her way in time. She *loved* this man, this Daniel. She was more than prepared to put up a good fight for him.

EPILOGUE

HER mirror told her she looked dazzling. This was the eve of her twenty-first birthday. A big party was being held downstairs in her honour. Moondai was a much healthier, happier place than it had been for many long years. Daniel continued to manage the station wonderfully but the time was rapidly approaching when she felt in her bones he would go to his grandfather. For Daniel with a good bit of coaxing from her had cemented his relationship with his grandfather. She could take extra credit for the fact Daniel had bowed to his grandfather's dearest wish to allow Moreland to be added to his name. These days Daniel was known as Daniel Carson-Moreland but everyone knew it was only a matter of time before the Carson was dropped. Maybe Daniel C. Moreland she'd suggested to him? She was after all, a terminal do-gooder.

The entire Outback had taken in its stride the revelation that Daniel Carson was actually Jared Moreland's son. Stories like that might have happened all the time for all the lack of fuss. The great thing was, Jared lived on in his son. Most were pretty sure a fine young man like the late Jared Moreland would have married his young love had he not lost his life so tragically and needlessly. Such a waste! But Daniel was universally liked and approved of, a fitting heir for his grandfather.

Neither Lloyd Kingston nor Berne resided at Moondai anymore. Berne was continuing his intensive training and doing extremely well. Lloyd had taken up residence in Perth, a city he had always liked, close to his academic friends. He had also acquired a lady friend he brought back with him to Moondai to celebrate Sandra's twenty-first. Festivities were to last the entire weekend. Sandra had invited all her old friends, especially those who had formed the hospital entertainment group. Vinnie, her former next door neighbour was invited, too.

Several members of the Moreland family had been invited, Sandra having met them on previous occasions. Sandra had taken to Cecile Moreland at once as Cecile had taken to her. It was very heartwarming to have such glad-hearted acceptance. It established them as friends who wanted to carry that friendship further. But then it was difficult not to be drawn to Cecile when she was so much like her cousin, Daniel.

Time to go downstairs! Sandra took one last look

at her reflection, aware there was the sheen of tears in her eyes. Excitement was running at full throttle, fuelling every fibre of her being.

And always and always... Daniel. If I'm beautiful, I'm beautiful for you!

Her cloud of hair had been tamed with exquisite, star shaped diamond pins, heirloom pieces from her grandmother, Catherine's, collection which was now hers. Her dress was truly lovely, very romantic, white chiffon hanging from shoestring straps, the bodice tightly draped, decorated with glittering beads, crystals and sequins, the skirt dreamy for dancing.

She inhaled deeply to calm those tumultuous nerves. *Oh, Daniel, please say you love me!* Didn't he know his name was written indelibly on her heart?

When they were together love seemed to be all around them, but still he hadn't spoken, true to his own standards. She knew his mother's trauma, left pregnant and quite alone to rear a fatherless child had affected him deeply. Responsibility was Daniel's middle name. She quite liked that really.

She was almost at the door when someone outside, knocked. Probably her mother. Her mother and her stepbrother, Michael were staying at the homestead, but she had gotten in early telling her mother she preferred it if her stepfather didn't come. Her mother had expressed dismay but Sandra had remained firm. Her stepfather would never be permitted to cross her threshold.

Only it was Daniel who was standing outside the door, looking marvellous but strangely tense.

"Oh, it's you!" Wherever he was, whenever he called, she would fly to him.

"Only me." He stared at her for the longest time, then barely containing his feelings breathed ardently, "You look a dream come true, birthday girl."

"Thank you, thank you." Colour bloomed in her cheeks. She smiled up at him, her eyes a burning violet-blue. "You look splendid too. How much did that dinner suit set you back?" she asked lightly, aware they were both highly emotional on this special night.

"I hired it."

"Did you really?" She studied the perfect fit, the set of his shoulders. "You didn't."

"Of course I didn't." He gave her his marvellous lopsided smile. "But I won't be able to afford another in a hurry. May I come in for a moment?"

"Certainly." She stood back to let him pass.

He paused in the centre of the room; turned to face her. "You've turned into a beautiful woman right in front of my eyes."

"You're saying I wasn't much to look at when you met me?" She adopted a teasing tone.

He laughed softly. "You were the prettiest youngster. But *not for long!*"

"I put my heart into getting beautiful, Daniel," she said. *All for you.*

"Well you made it," he said, with considerable feeling, thrusting a hand inside his dinner jacket.

"What are you doing?" Her voice wobbled.

"I'm giving you your birthday present now, okay?" He looked up, a silver flame in his eyes.

"I just hope it cost a lot of money," she tried to joke. "Just fooling, Daniel."

"I know. That was one big fat cheque you wrote for the Childhood Leukaemia Foundation."

She nodded her satisfaction. "Joel has agreed to match me. I really love him, you know. My grandad didn't inspire a lot of affection. Your grandad is the kind of man one loves."

"He is," Daniel agreed with obvious affection, then with sudden intensity, "What about *me?*"

"I've told you I love you a number of times. I won't be tempted again."

"So I'll send this back then?" he asked, waving a small velvet box about.

"After I've seen what it is." A swarm of butterflies took flight in her stomach.

He moved towards her with his characteristic athletic grace, going down on one knee. "I've got to do this properly." He looked up at her with half smiling, but deeply serious eyes. "Alexandra Mary Kingston," he said with burning formality, "would you do me the great honour of becoming my wife?" He didn't wait for an answer but put out his arms and gripped her slender body to him. "Darling Sandra,

I never had a life before you. You have to marry me."

She couldn't answer at once, literally speechless with joy. "Oh, Daniel, you're going to make me cry," she whispered, her two hands cupping his beloved head. "I dare not. I'll spoil my makeup. Oh, Daniel, I never believed you'd ask me."

He rose to his feet, bending to kiss the creamy slope of her shoulder. "How could you not?" he asked gently. "You know how *I* feel just as I know how *you* feel. We love each other. We were meant for each other since we were born." Swiftly he opened the box in his hand. "Here is my gift to you, your engagement ring. It comes with my solemn promise to love, honour and protect you all my life. Give me your hand, sweetheart."

Sandra raised it, but overcome by emotion, squeezed her eyes shut. Precious metal slipped down her finger.

"You can open your eyes now," Daniel said in a gentle loving voice.

"Oh, Daniel!" She stared down at her precious ring, a glorious sapphire flanked by baguette diamonds. "I feel like I'm going to bawl my eyes out."

"Not now, you can't," he reminded her. "You can cry in my arms when the party is over."

"Is that a promise? I don't think I can contain myself so long."

"Well we have to. I don't dare muss you, you look

perfect. Tears, lots of cuddles and kisses are allowed later, but though it's *excruciating* and a real test of my control, we're not going to bed together. Not until the first night of our honeymoon which I personally guarantee will be the most wonderful night of our lives. Do you trust me?"

She smiled radiantly. "Trust in you wraps me like a security blanket. I've always trusted you, Daniel. From the moment I laid eyes on you at the airport. Now, having said that, I don't want to pester you, but *when* is this honeymoon going to be? It's a good time to put pressure on you because I don't mind telling you I'm in an agony of longing."

"You think *I'm* not?" He linked his arms around the waist. "I'm ready to start it *immediately,* but what I want even more is to see you as my shining bride. The woman I love and honour. That said, what about as soon as possible in the New Year? Would a few months give you enough time to get organised? I don't think we're going to get out of a big wedding, do you?"

"The biggest!" In an ecstasy of joy she started to whirl around the room all the while holding her beautiful engagement ring up to the light.

"Like it?" He caught her to him, commanding her to a stop.

"Love it. Love you."

"That's what I want to hear." He allowed himself several kisses that trailed from behind one small ear, down the column of her throat to her shoulder, all the while inhaling the lovely perfume she wore. "There couldn't be any question as to the stone," he said huskily. "A perfect sapphire outmatched by your eyes."

"Are you going to kiss me anywhere else?" she whispered.

His brilliant eyes rested on her mouth. "Don't tempt me. One kiss and it would all get out of hand as you very well know. We'll store the kisses up until the early hours of your birthday morning. Meanwhile I'll kiss those delicate fingers." He brought her hand to his mouth, running the tip of his tongue over her smooth knuckles.

"Daniel," she said weakly, just about ready to dissolve.

"This is *nothing* to what I'm going to do to you," he told her in a low thrilling voice.

"I *know!*" She gave an expectant shiver. "I'm going to pieces already."

"Me, too!" Ardently he touched a finger to the little pulse that beat in the hollow of her throat. "We'll have a lifetime together, Sandra." His voice was full of the wonder of being deeply, truly in love. "Just think of it!"

An enormous lightness of being seized Sandra. She linked her arm through his as they walked to the door. "From this day forward!"

"From this day forward," he repeated, looking down at her with his spirit, exultant, in his eyes. "You and me on life's journey."

For a long lovely moment they were sealed off in a world of their own.

I'm getting what every woman prays for, Sandra thought, an expression of utter bliss irradiating her face. I'm getting the thing in life that really matters: Having a wonderful man love me as I love him.

Only with Daniel could this happen.

* * * * *

THE HEIR'S CHOSEN BRIDE *by Marion Lennox*

As a widow and single mum, Susan is wary about meeting
Hamish Douglas, the man who has inherited the castle where
she and her small daughter live. Surely he'll want to sell up?
Hamish had planned to turn the castle into a luxury hotel
– until he met the beautiful Susie…

THE MILLIONAIRE'S CINDERELLA WIFE
by Lilian Darcy

Many women lust after millionaire Ty Garrett. Sierra has one
problem with that – he is her husband! Sierra wants a divorce
– but Ty has a suggestion. To deter all the lusting females
will Sierra stay for a while? Will she give their love a second
chance?

THEIR UNFINISHED BUSINESS *by Jackie Braun*

Even after ten years Ali Conlan's heart still beat strongly for
the man who had left her – and her body still responded to his
bad-boy confidence and winning smile. His visit to Trillium
was for business…but perhaps they could resolve their own
unfinished business?

THE TYCOON'S PROPOSAL *by Leigh Michaels*

When Lissa Morgan takes a two-week live-in job, she doesn't
realise that she will be in close proximity to Kurt Callahan
– the man who had broken her heart years before when she
discovered he had dated her for a bet! Can Lissa forgive and
forget…?

On sale 7th July 2006

*Available at WHSmith, Tesco, ASDA, Borders, Eason,
Sainsbury's and most bookshops*

www.millsandboon.co.uk

Look for these exciting new titles on Mills & Boon Audio CDs on sale from 5th May 2006

The Greek's Chosen Wife by Lynne Graham
Wife Against Her Will by Sara Craven

A Practical Mistress by Mary Brendan
The Gladiator's Honour by Michelle Styles

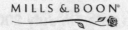

www.millsandboon.co.uk

4 Books
and a surprise gift!

We would like to take this opportunity to thank you for reading this Mills & Boon® book by offering you the chance to take FOUR more specially selected titles from the Tender Romance™ series absolutely FREE! We're also making this offer to introduce you to the benefits of the Reader Service™—

* ★ FREE home delivery
* ★ FREE gifts and competitions
* ★ FREE monthly Newsletter
* ★ Exclusive Reader Service offers
* ★ Books available before they're in the shops

Accepting these FREE books and gift places you under no obligation to buy, you may cancel at any time, even after receiving your free shipment. Simply complete your details below and return the entire page to the address below. You don't even need a stamp!

YES! Please send me 4 free Tender Romance books and a surprise gift. I understand that unless you hear from me, I will receive 6 superb new titles every month for just £2.80 each, postage and packing free. I am under no obligation to purchase any books and may cancel my subscription at any time. The free books and gift will be mine to keep in any case.

N6ZEE

Ms/Mrs/Miss/Mr ....Initials ....
BLOCK CAPITALS PLEASE

Surname ....

Address ....

....

....Postcode ....

Send this whole page to:
UK: FREEPOST CN81, Croydon, CR9 3WZ